"LONGARM! BEHIND YOU!"

He spun, as most men would have, to see that a shorter, somewhat older man he recognized at a glance, had seen him first and already slapped leather!

A single shot rang out.

Then it got very quiet in the Silver Dollar Saloon as the other man stared owl-eyed at Longarm through the gunsmoke hanging in the air betwixt them as Longarm held his fire, calmly saying, "Evening, Mister Sinclair. Long time no see."

The seriously wanted Fuzzy Sinclair croaked, "How . . . did . . . you . . . do . . . that?" before his knees crumpled and he fell at Longarm's feet, dead as a turd in a milk bucket.

DON'T MISS THESE
ALL-ACTION WESTERN SERIES
FROM THE BERKLEY PUBLISHING GROUP

THE GUNSMITH by J. R. Roberts
Clint Adams was a legend among lawmen, outlaws and ladies.
They called him . . . the Gunsmith.

LONGARM by Tabor Evans
The popular long-running series about Deputy U.S. Marshal
Long—his life, his loves, his fight for justice.

SLOCUM by Jake Logan
Today's longest-running action Western. John Slocum rides
a deadly trail of hot blood and cold steel.

BUSHWHACKERS by B. J. Lanagan
An action-packed series by the creators of *Longarm!* The
rousing adventures of the most brutal gang of cutthroats ever
assembled—Quantrill's Raiders.

DIAMONDBACK by Guy Brewer
Dex Yancey is Diamondback, a Southern gentleman turned
con man when his brother cheats him out of the family fortune. Ladies love him. Gamblers hate him. But nobody pulls
one over on Dex . . .

WILDGUN by Jack Hanson
The blazing adventures of mountain man Will Barlow—from
the creators of *Longarm!*

TEXAS TRACKER by Tom Calhoun
Meet J. T. Law: the most relentless—and dangerous—man-
hunter in all Texas. Where sheriffs and posses fail, he's the
best man to bring in the most vicious outlaws—for a price.

TABOR EVANS

LONGARM

AND THE
AMOROUS AMAZON

JOVE BOOKS, NEW YORK

This is a work of fiction. Names, characters, places, and incidents either are the product of the author's imagination or are used fictitiously, and any resemblance to actual persons, living or dead, business establishments, events, or locales is entirely coincidental.

LONGARM AND THE AMOROUS AMAZON

A Jove Book / published by arrangement with the author

PRINTING HISTORY
Jove edition / November 2002

Copyright © 2002 by Penguin Putnam Inc.

Visit our website at
www.penguinputnam.com

ISBN: 0-515-13406-6

A JOVE BOOK®
Jove Books are published by The Berkley Publishing Group, a division of Penguin Putnam Inc., 375 Hudson Street, New York, New York 10014.
JOVE and the "J" design are trademarks belonging to Penguin Putnam Inc.

PRINTED IN THE UNITED STATES OF AMERICA

10 9 8 7 6 5 4 3 2 1

Chapter 1

When a man is fixing to hang come Monday morning, he dosen't sleep too soundly on Saturday night. So the Fargo Kid became aware of the fuss out front before it made its way back to the cell block of the Pueblo County Jail to find him wide awake and upright with his hands on the bars of his cage.

The Fargo Kid would never see thirty again, but he hadn't grown worth a mention since he'd killed a Wells Fargo shotgun messenger out California way, at the age of seventeen. So he still struck some at first glance as a runty juvenile delinquent who'd led a hard life. Standing five foot two in his high-heeled Justins, he had to stare soberly up at what seemed a gigantic woman or a mighty big sissy in a dark velvet riding habit with a perky veiled derby pinned atop upswept auburn hair. The voice sounded she-male enough as she gestured with the eighteen inches of bloody blade in one hand and the ring of keys in her other to ask the prisoner, soberly, "What would you do to get out of here, young sir?"

To which the Fargo Kid could only reply, "You name it, and if it's humanly possible you got it, ma'am. Did I think I had a soul, I'd be proud to pledge it to you and the other demons in exchange for my mortal neck!"

The monstrous woman said they had a deal as she unlocked the cage door to add, "Follow me tight and watch your step out front. You'll find the floor a bit slippery."

As the Fargo Kid followed, a plaintive voice from three cells down called, "Hey, Lady, what about me?"

The towering woman spun with a poker face to reply, "What about who? They told me Fargo was alone back here!"

The Fargo Kid soothed, "They told you true, ma'am. He's nobody. Just an old drunk they toss in yonder cell every Saturday night to keep him from scaring horses along Union Avenue. He ain't with us."

She moved that way, softly chiding, "Don't be such a snob, dear heart. Would you have me let a fellow mortal spend this night in jail when I have all these swell keys to play with?"

As the killer who'd been waiting on the county hangman followed with a bemused expression, she moved with surprising grace for one so large to let the second prisoner out. As she unlocked his cell door, the shabby sot allowed she was an angel sent from heaven to save him from a Saturday night of sobriety. Then he was making odd gurgling noises as he writhed at her feet, clutching at the throat she'd slashed from ear to ear in a motion too swift for the Fargo Kid to follow!

As she herded him the other way with a wave of that blood-slicked bowie, the smaller killer gasped, "Jesus H. Christ, ma'am. How come you did that? He was only a harmless drunk!"

She calmly replied, "So now he's a dead harmless drunk, and dead men tell no tales. Didn't that murder trial you just had teach you anything about witnesses, my child? I was only following your misadventures in the *Rocky Mountain News*, but it did seem to me they'd have

2

never convicted you if friends you'd counted on hadn't turned you in for the price on your trusting head."

The Fargo Kid's face was not a pretty sight to see as he followed the gigantic woman out to the better light of the front office. He saw the shades were down. He was glad they were as he took in her bloody version of the last act of *Hamlet* and muttered, "*Slippery* is a sort of understatement, ma'am! How in thunder did you get the drop on the both of them with just that bowie, slick as you seem to carve with it?"

As they circled the body sprawled across the booking desk to step over another, spread-eagled on the blood-slicked floor, she modestly replied, "It was easy. I'm a girl. As I was shyly filing my complaint about a fresh drunk, they were both standing close with concern, and as you may have noticed, I have quite a reach for a woman. But let's talk about that later. We have to get you out of here and safely out of human ken before anyone notices what we've done, here."

The Fargo Kid almost said something rude. But as she trimmed the lamp by the front door, he reflected on how, from the point of view of that hangman, it hardly mattered who'd done what to whom, now.

She didn't have to tell him how dousing the light inside was sure to attract attention. It was more important that nobody out front at that hour describe them in detail as they stepped out to walk, not run, directly across the street to the darkened entrance of a hat shop closed for the night. As she tossed the key ring from the jail back the way they'd just come, she produced another key to unlock the door of the hat shop, murmuring, "Follow me tight, and don't mess anything in passing through in the dark. We don't want the old dears who run this shop in the daylight to know how this novelty shop skeleton key fits their cheap pedestrian lock, do we?"

"I reckon not." The much shorter Fargo Kid grinned as

3

he followed her not unattractive bulk through the gloom, once she'd locked the front door after them. She seemed to know the way. He didn't ask how come. As an experienced rider of the owlhoot trail, he could see how easy it would be for a flighty she-male customer to ask to use the outhouse in the back yard and be treated to a guided tour of the facilities at an earlier date.

Leading him out the back and locking up, the ominously graceful figure in dark velvet guided him past the two holer he'd expected and out a back gate to a cinder-paved alleyway, softly assuring him they were almost there.

"Almost where, ma'am?" he asked in a worried tone, adding, "We got to get far and wide before they notice that mess . . . we left back yonder and raise the hue and cry! I figure we have mayhaps four hours of darkness left, and, with any luck and sudden horses, that only adds up to a thirty mile lead, tops, before they can read our trail by the dawn's early light, right?"

"Wrong," she replied with a weary sigh, adding, "That pony express wore a pony out for the day after a fifteen mile lope, little man. No horse born to mortal damn is about to carry a rider *my* size more than six miles at a lope before I need a fresh mount or a good long trail break. But don't you imagine they'll think we left by *rail* when they fail to miss any horses here in the county seat, come that cold gray dawn?"

As she suddenly opened another back gate in the tricky light, they both heard a not too distant railroad whistle, and the Fargo Kid said, "Do Jesus! I follow your drift, and how in thunder did a gal so young and pretty get so fiendishly clever, ma'am?"

She demurely replied, "The last ten years in prison were very, very educational. They call me Increase Younger and I copped a plea to robbery to avoid the charge of murder in the first. Stick with me and I'll show *you* how

4

to get away with murder, Fargo. But pipe down, now, lest my new neighbors wonder about such an innocent damsel sneaking a man into her hired cottage at this ungodly hour!"

He followed and made no comments while she guided him not through another *back* door but down through a slanted *cellar* door into total darkness that smelled of cobwebs, coal dust and potatoes.

She warned, "Take my hand. We don't strike a match at this hour, but we're almost home free!"

The Fargo Kid hadn't been getting any since they'd arrested him eight weeks back, and so while her hand was bigger than his by far, the Fargo Kid was hard-pressed to recall a softer more she-male paw, as deadly as this one might be!

As if reading his mind, she murmured, "Down, boy. We have to see to your staying alive before we worry about your other feelings! Watch your step. There's a sort of Chinese doorsill ahead."

As his boot tip thudded against an ankle-high plank set on edge, he followed her drift as well as her grip through a mysterious opening into cleaner-smelling darkness scented slightly with . . . strawberries?

She told him to stay put, and he heard her sliding a heavy wooden mass into place with a dull thud before she said, "Good. Now let's have some light on the subject."

She struck a match. As she applied it to an oil lamp on a kitchen table, the Fargo Kid saw they were in a windowless room paneled with knotty pine on one side. Three other walls were of red sandstone set crudely with gray portland mortar. Aside from the table and sideboard piled with food and drink, there stood two camp chairs and a brass bedstead heaped with linen bedding and Hudson Bay blankets. As the Fargo Kid was taking all this in, Increase Younger was taking off her hat and dark velvet habit, demurely observing, "I chose velvet this dark because blood splatters tend to soak in. But all in all, I think we'd better burn it, now."

The Fargo Kid was certain of her gender, now. For even wearing her chemise and petticoat, there was enough of her spilling over to once more remind the Fargo Kid he hadn't been getting any, lately.

Unpinning her long auburn hair to let it fall becomingly around her creamy, albeit massive, bare shoulders, the towering vision of she-male pulchritude tossed her blood-splattered disguise in a nail keg in one corner to don a kimono of ivory Turkish toweling as she told her confounded guest to sit down, adding, "I have to be topside in case anyone comes calling. They're likely to canvas for blocks around that jail once they find the place so untidy. If you hear boot heels on the floorboards above just sit tight. Nobody will ever know you're down here as long as you don't announce it at the top of your lungs."

"Where am I?" He demanded, dubiously.

Fastening the sash of her kimono, Increase confided, "Behind a false wall I built all by my little self behind shelves I put up to hold all that fruit I've preserved upstairs since I got out of prison a few weeks ago. One gets the same effect by washing the labels off store-bought preserves. The point is that the overall effect is a solid cellar wall to the eye of any caller without a set of house plans. You *do* know how to play hide-and-seek without sneezing or laughing out loud, don't you?"

He grinned to reply, "I reckon. You sure have been busy since you got out of prison, ma'am. Would you care to tell me, now, why you've gone to so much plotting and planning on my behalf, considering we've never met before, and I have caught occasional glances of myself in a mirror I just couldn't avoid!"

She waved him to a seat on the feather mattress as she sighed and said, "I try to avoid mirrors as well. Everyone in my family runs to size, and you men are so silly about

6

girls you have to look up to. I chose you for my partner in a matter of mutual pleasure for several reasons. To begin with, I knew without having to ask that you'd be willing to go along with my plans. After that, I knew where you would *be* while I made our opening moves. Nobody had any call to suspect I was out to rescue you before this very night. There was nothing to connect me or mine with you and yours when I arrived in town a few weeks ago to set this hideout up. I had all the time I needed to shop for all the stuff I needed to fashion this secret room behind all my swell home preserves.

"Yesterday, knowing I'd be saving you this evening from that hanging come Monday morn, I took a local train over to Avondale to drop a letter from you in a mailbox near the depot. It won't be postmarked and sent back up the line from Avondale before Monday, when you would have hanged, had the law and your false friends had their way. I took the liberty of having you rub that in as you warn Crimp Gooding his own days are now numbered. I wrote the letter on a G & S typewriting machine and didn't sign your name lest an old pal question your signature. I'm sure Crimp Gooding will be able to guess who the death threats will be coming from, don't you?"

He nodded soberly but said, "Crimp's only one on my long list of false-hearted friends in these parts. But to tell the pure truth, I ain't sure I should have sent that letter, no offense. For wouldn't Crimp Gooding and my other false friends be on the prod *before* such a letter arrived, just knowing I'd cheated the noose them sons of bitches had tried to put around my poor neck?"

She calmly replied, "Of course they'll be watching out for you in *these* parts. That's why nobody will be watching for you up to the state capital after they try in vain to cut your trail in Avondale."

"We're headed for Denver, Miss Increase?" he replied uncertainly.

7

She said, "You are. By way of a northbound combination leaving Pueblo shortly after the county law heads east to Avondale to bring you back. Nobody will be expecting anybody who looks like *me* to hunt down *your* enemies here in Pueblo County. They'll be on guard against a familiar little squirt they know on sight at a distance, no offense."

As the penny dropped, the Fargo Kid grinned like a fox in a henhouse to chortle, "I follow your drift, and, no offense to *you*, Miss Increase, you're about the last thing Crimp Gooding, Mel Stuart and that double-crossing Trixie Davis might fear at first glance. But why are you being so good to me, you purdly little thing?"

She thoughtfully untied the sash of her kimono as she decided, "We may have time to satisfy *that* mutual hunger before I have to get it on upstairs to cover for us. I've just spent ten of my most womanly years in prison, and that Trixie you used to sleep with has been with Crimp Gooding since he talked her into betraying you, right?"

As she calmly continued to strip, the Fargo Kid gasped, "Lord have mercy if you don't have a whole lot to offer a man, Miss Increase! But I'd be fibbing if I said you had to do *that* to steal a kiss!"

As she tossed the kimono aside and proceeded to shuck her chemise, the towering vision of heroic femininity said, "I want more than a kiss. Take off your clothes!"

As he started to, fumble-fingered with mingled desire and astonishment, she continued, "I know I'm not so old and ugly I have to kill folk to get laid. I've fucked one man after the other since I got out of prison last month, and I'm still not half satisfied. But I won't be killing Crimp Gooding, Trixie Davis and Mel Stuart because you're yet another horny soul. If you want me to kill for you here in Pueblo County, you'll have to kill just one old enemy of *mine*, up the line in Denver. Agreed?"

As she tossed aside the petticoat to boldly face him,

hands on hips, stark naked, the Fargo Kid gasped, "Only *one*? Great day in the morning if I wouldn't be proud to gun a *dozen* men down for a pal like *you*!"

So she flopped down beside him as he popped shirt buttons to mount her with his pants down around his boot tops, sobbing in pure lust as he entered her surprisingly tight delights. So a fine time was had by all, and it was a good quarter hour before he got around to asking her who she wanted him to kill up Denver way.

Hugging her to him with her massive thighs, Increase Younger kissed him some more before she told him, "The man who shot my brother while I was in prison. A Deputy U.S. Marshal Custis Long. You may have heard-tell of him. They call him Longarm."

Chapter 2

Since every Saturday night must wind down to a Sunday morning, the dawn's early light found Deputy U.S. Marshal Custis Long of the Denver District Court having breakfast at an all-night chili parlor on Larimer Street after an unusual night in bed by himself.

As he broke fast at the stand-up counter near the livery stable he meant to visit next, the tall, tanned West Virginian in a tobacco tweed suit worn over army stovepipes and a cross-draw gunbelt was joined by a somewhat older and way shorter figure in a more expensive black gabardine outfit. Marshal Billy Vail growled past the stubby black stogie betwixt his teeth, "Morning, old son, they told me you were planning on squiring that new gal from the federal building to that Sunday-go-on-the-green, so I figured to catch you down this way before you hired that buggy over yonder."

Longarm, as he was better known as far south as Pueblo of late, sighed. "Boss, it's my only day of rest, and they told you wrong about that new gal at the office. I had it in mind to drive this store-keeping gal you never heard of out to that Methodist campground this morning."

Billy Vail said, "Oh, her? Smarter move than messing

with pussy where you're paid. I didn't head you off like this to chide you about your love life, old son. Got a telegram late last night too late to risk disturbing your love life. Increase Younger got out of prison last month. She's been seen since, here in Colorado. So she might have meant some of the things she wrote you in that letter."

As the colored counter hand slid his plate of chili con carne under two fried eggs his way, Longarm nodded his thanks, allowed he'd take his coffee with his grub, and turned back to his boss to say, "I must not be awake yet. If we're talking about a gal with a peculiar name for anybody, I don't recall getting any letters from her of late."

Billy Vail smiled sheepishly and said, "Didn't want to worry you over nothing, old son. You've no idea how many death threats you get, sent in care of my office. Henry, out front, opens all the mail, and so he naturally shows me anything he feels I ought to know about."

As the counter hand placed a mug of black joe by his breakfast, Longarm dryly remarked, "It's nice to know you and Henry save me so much bother. Did this Miss Increase Younger say how come she means to do me harm?"

Vail flatly replied, "She means to kill you because you killed her brother, *Cotton* Younger. Remember him?"

Longarm grimaced and replied, "A man that size would be hard to forget if I hadn't shot it out with him in a Utah courthouse in front of the judge. He'd changed his name but they called him Timberline because he hadn't been able to hide the simple fact that he was a head taller than me and I ain't exactly a shrimp. You'd sent me after him because he was said to be kin to them other Youngers riding with Frank and Jesse in their Northfield raid back in '76."

"That may have been a false lead," Vail conceded, adding, "Even as we speak, Cole Younger and his two kid brothers languish in the Minnesota state prison. All three deny any known kinship to what they describe as a more trashy Younger clan. There's no need to bring you up-to-date on the treacherous and deadly Cotton Younger or those other associates who wound up just as dead whilst trying to avenge him, more recent. So allow me to introduce you to Cotton Younger's literally big sister, Miss Increase Younger, age thirty-seven, height six foot six, weight about two-fifty but well distributed over more muscle than the average man might boast. After that she's described as almost pretty for a gal or mighty handsome for a man, with naturally blond hair she tends to darken with the aid of modern chemistry. As her name might indicate, she and her baby brother, Cotton, were baptised and raised by strict Calvinists. It didn't rub off on either. But they both inherited the family tendency to run to size."

Vail shifted the cigar stub in his mouth to sort of muse, "Some say criminal natures are inherited whilst others blame the potato famine, the war or whatever. Suffice it to say Increase introduced her younger siblings to petty crime and some say serious sex at an early age. She was sent to prison before you ever came to work for me, six or eight years ago. So she had nothing to do with the charges we had on her bad-enough brother. She read about you shooting it out with him, though, and seems to have taken it hard. Her death threat was postmarked Kansas City. Earlier this month, she was arrested in Jimtown, Colorado."

Longarm washed down some more of his breakfast with bitter black coffee before he demanded, "How come?" in a bemused tone.

Vail said, "On suspicion, of course. The spectacular gal towers over the average crowd and Jimtown's a gold camp plagued by whores and gamblers of all sizes and descriptions. They run the big flashy gal in for an overnight all-points and had to let her go when they found out the prison release she'd showed them was real. She declined to say how she'd come by the fancy outfit or wad of greenbacks they'd picked her up with. The state of Iowa had only turned her loose with two dollars and a cheap new dress, but . . ."

"I meant how come it was Jimtown, up by Trapper's Rock, if she'd come out our way after me, here in Denver."

Vail shrugged and decided, "She means to circle in, most likely. I just told you she stood out in a crowd and . . ."

Longarm hastily swallowed to cut in, "That makes no sense! If you stood out in a crowd, no offense, would you send advance warning and then try to pussyfoot in on the one you'd just declared war upon?"

Vail grimaced, not a pretty sight, and tried, "She's established herself as crazy-mean. She can't be thinking as clear as you and me or she'd know better than to to come after any lawman in any fashion after just doing ten at hard for gunning yet another poor cuss who'd only been trying to do his job."

Longarm demanded, "She only drew ten at hard for gunning a man? She must be good-looking indeed!"

Vail explained, "She copped a plea. It was uncertain which member of her three-man gang plugged that bank guard. A surviving witness said it was her, but her two followers went down in the running gunfight that followed, and she cried so convincingly in court that they decided to settle for what they had her cold on. She said, and they chose to believe, she'd only been scouting for bank robbers who'd forced her to go in ahead and . . ."

"It seems to me I've heard that song before," Longarm cut in as he caught the counter hand's eye and pointed at his empty mug. As soon as he saw his signal had been received, he told Vail, "Let's say this Miss Increase

14

Younger thinks on her feet and changes her story to fit the way the wind is blowing. Let's not waste time pondering how even an ugly woman who'd fuck a baby brother might have come by any amount of money since getting out of prison. Let's worry about where she went after they let her out up Jimtown way!"

Vail said, "Worry is the word I was searching for. She or at least a mighty tall blond checked in and out of the Dexter Hotel, handy to the Union Station, just last week. But she was gone before we and the Denver P.D. could get a line on her. So I can't say for certain she was Increase Younger instead of another big old blond."

As he tasted his fresh mug to find it just as strong and black, Longarm dryly remarked, "*Now* he tells me. Were you fixing to tell me somebody was gunning for me at my funeral, Uncle Billy?"

Vail soothed, "Like I said, you get death threats all the time, and I didn't want you distracted on the job. I'm telling you now, and you ain't dead yet, are you?"

Longarm laughed despite himself and said, "You're right. I do find myself more worried about Cotton Younger's mighty big sister than that courthouse chore come Monday morn or, come to study on it, another lady I was fixing to escort to a Sunday-go-to-meeting-on-the-green."

"You'd best cut down on your social life until we get a handle on this other gal out to kill you," Vail warned. "It wouldn't be right to risk another gal's life like that. If I were you, I'd just forget about driving out to the Methodist campgrounds with your pretty Miss Alvina."

"You ain't me," sighed Longarm, making a mental note that the gossips had been reporting his moves on Miss Alvina Witherspoon to Billy Vail's old woman up on Sherman Street as he added, "When I tell a lady I mean to pick her up at her house at nine A.M. I don't mean Lord willing and the creeks don't rise. Even as we speak the poor little gal we're speaking of has doubtless had a bath whether she needed one or not and fluffed up the summer frock she means to wear out yonder."

Vail said, "Custis, that other woman is a cold-blooded killer, and she nailed that bank guard with one shot!"

Longarm nodded but pointed out, "After which you just told me she stands six foot six, and they're holding the revival meeting and cake sale on open prairie south of the current city limits. Even if such an outstanding personality knows my social plans on my day off, how do you reckon she plans to sneak up on me in broad-ass daylight over all that shin-deep grama and buffalo grass?"

He saw he wasn't getting through and added, "You were right to hold back crank mail meant to worry my mind, boss. How would I get anything done around here if I took every death threat serious?"

Vail insisted, "Increase Younger ain't no crank. Increase Younger is a killer, treacherous as a Jezebel crossed with a wolverine! And we do have her hovering about, just off-stage!"

Longarm shook his head to say, "All six foot six of her and nary a thing to charge her with when we spot her unless she's willing to own up to that letter she may or may not have sent."

Vail snorted, "Shit, who *else* would have writ from Kansas City in her name, for Pete's sake?"

"Somebody who didn't like her," Longarm easily replied as he fished in his pants for some change and said, "I can't be the only one who's made enemies over the years, and she's killed others as well. So what if somebody *else* is out to make trouble for the both of us? Kansas City ain't in line to Denver from Iowa and . . ."

"I just told you she was circling in on you!" Vail flared.

But Longarm insisted, "Did she circle in to belly up to this counter and order breakfast, there'd be nothing either one of us could do about it before and until she makes

16

one unlawful move! Ain't no law against a lady who's just got out of prison in Iowa enjoying the scenery of Colorado for a change. You've warned me to be on guard around her, and I mean to be on guard around her if ever I lay eyes on her, boss. But in the meantime I have other fish to fry. So do you need a lift back up the hill to your place?"

Vail said he'd tethered his own Tennessee walker out front. So Longarm nodded at the counter hand and left a modest tip as they stepped away to amble out front. Some held you had no call to tip at a stand-up counter. But Longarm broke fast there often, and they'd never stinted on the chili beans or charged him for his usual extra coffee, and so, like they said, when you took care of folk, they most often took care of you.

They parted friendly but still fussing out front, and Longarm went across to the livery to hire two mules and a Studebaker buggy with an oilcloth canopy. Then he drove it on down to Alvina Witherspoon's quarters above the carriage house behind the medical supply shop she ran, a spit and a holler east of Denver General. Alvina Witherspoon was not a trained nurse or a Sister. But she dressed like one behind the counter of her shop. So Longarm wasn't certain what she'd be wearing out to the campgrounds that morning.

Once he'd tethered his hired team downstairs and gone up to knock, the petite blue-eyed brunette in question opened up in her navy blue bathrobe to state, accusingly, "Custis! I wasn't expecting you for an hour! I just got out of my bath and . . . Heavens, come on in before the neighbors see me standing here in such a state of deshabille!"

As he followed her in, removing his telescoped coffee-brown Stetson, Longarm soothed, "Aw, you don't look too disabled, Miss Alvina. I'm here early because I didn't want you getting all gussied up if you don't want to ride out to that Sunday-go with me, this morning."

17

She whirled about, looking hurt as she demanded, "What are you talking about? Don't you *want* to be seen in public with me, Custis Long?"

"I don't care how many residents of Denver might see us together in public," he lied. "But before you even powder that perky little nose, we got to talk about a certain lady who might have just blown in from Iowa."

"Oh?" the Denver brunette replied in a desperately cool tone, to add, three degrees cooler, "Does she have a name, and who might she be to you, Deputy Long?"

He told her, truthfully this time, "Her given name is Miss Increase Younger, and I've yet to lay eyes on her. She just got out of the Iowa state prison after doing ten at hard for armed robbery and worse. I shot her brother in Utah a spell back, and now that she's out and free to move about, she seems to be headed our way, all six foot six of her. My boss, Marshal Vail, thinks she's after me. My boss could be right. I hope he's wrong, but you've a right to know things could get noisy in my vicinity if a letter sent in her name is to be taken at all serious. Now it's your turn."

Alvina stared up goggle-eyed to say, "Ooh, this is so exciting! You'd told me not to believe those tales about you in the *Rocky Mountain News* but now I see they must be true! You have to hide, here with me, until we find out whether that horrible woman means to assassinate you or not. Come back to my boudoir so we can get out of this ridiculous vertical position as we plan for your very survival, you poor dear!"

As he followed Longarm almost said he doubted a six-foot-six blond would find it easy to sneak up on him. Then he wondered why any man would want to say such a dumb thing to another lady leading the way into her bedroom.

Chapter 3

A hundred-odd miles to the south, a way bigger gal was leading a somewhat shorter lawman into her own boudoir, dressed for such an occasion in a fresh kimono of Turkish toweling. Waving an expansive hand at the rumpled bedding she demurely told her own morning visitor, "I told you I spent a restless night alone in this house, Deputy Manx. What on earth was all that yelling and galloping through the wee small hours about?"

Uncomfortably aware of the musky body odors given off by the huge but hardly undesirable woman of some maturity, Deputy Roy Manx of Pueblo County said, "I thought I told you, ma'am, we had us a serious jailbreak not more than a skip and a holler from here. I would have took your word when you said you dwelt here alone. The sheriff only said to canvas about for anyone who might have seen the two rascals."

She purred, "Let me show you through the rest of the place. You'll see I have nothing to hide. You say you're looking for *two* escaped prisoners, sir?"

As she led him back to the kitchen, Manx said, "One prisoner and a pal or more who busted him out. I know that don't sound like much, but the one they busted out

19

was fixing to hang for murder, come Monday morn, and they murdered two lawmen and the town drunk as they saved his neck last night."

Increase Younger opened the door to the cellar steps, and she said she could see why they wanted to catch such a desperate gang. Then she suggested, "We'd best make certain they're not hiding in my cellar. I have some matches and a candlestick handly, somewhere in here. But I fear you've made me uneasy with your talk about a gang of killers on the loose here in Pueblo. Maybe you ought to go first as I light the way?"

Roy Manx said he'd be proud to lead the way as he drew his S & W double-action with a flourish. It wasn't easy, but Increase managed not to laugh at the kid as she stuck a light to hold the candle high while he proceeded down the steps ahead of her, waving the muzzle of his six-gun at the shifting shadows. He was a nice looking boy, and so easy to lead by the nose. Increase Younger liked that in a man.

Down below, as she'd expected, the younger lawman made a show of sweeping the deliberately cluttered cellar for escaped outlaws until he came to the standing wall of pickles and preserves. Just as she'd assured the smaller man cowering behind it with his own cocked six-gun, the lawman whistled in admiration to declare, "You surely do have a heap of relish and dessert down here, ma'am. But do you mind if I ask how come? Lady next door says you just moved in."

Thinking fast, the big blond with auburn hair purred, "We're going to have to watch how we behave in front of such nosey neighbors, won't we? A lot of the stuff you see down here was left behind by the last tenants. I didn't want to make a fuss about it. I was anxious to move in, and, as you just said, some of those jars look tempting. Would you like to have a jar of jam, or mayhaps some pickled melon rind?"

The lawman smiled boyishly to reply, "Lord love you, ma'am, my wife and kids would surely go for some watermelon pickles or a jar of apple butter. But I'm supposed to be canvassing, not shopping for groceries, so . . ."

"Come back later, once you get off duty," she suggested, adding, "I have errands of my own, and I haven't been to church yet. But you'll find me here, anxious for company in a strange town, if you'd care to come by after suppertime this evening."

Roy Manx allowed he'd be proud to come by and relieve her of some lonely feelings and a few jars from those crowded shelves. So they went back upstairs, and she told him to call her Creasy if she could call him Roy. So they shook on it and then, locking eyes, they kissed on it. But as the deputy tried to run his gun hand under her kimono, she softly warned, "Not yet, Roy. Give a girl time to think. You did say you were a married man, didn't you?"

He sheepishly replied, "Nobody feels all that married when he meets up with a gal purdy as *you*, Miss Creasy."

Then he tried to kiss her again and she let him, giving him just a hint of tongue before she pushed him away, being stronger by far, to shyly murmur, "I said I needed time to think. We'll talk about it later this evening, Roy."

He said they surely would and left, whistling.

Once she'd locked up after him, Increase went back down to rejoin her hidden guest. She found the Fargo Kid half dressed behind the false end of the confusing cellar, hauling on a second boot as he half sobbed up at her, "Have you lost your mind, girl? Why the hell did you have to invite that lawman back tonight? Are you trying to get us caught? Have you forgot it was you, not me, who carved three men dead at the county jail less than twenty-four hours ago?"

She secured the secret sliding door and calmly shucked her kimono to stride over to the bed stark naked as she soothed, "I aim to shack up with him. Don't get your

21

bowels in an uproar, dear heart. I'm all yours until it's safe for you to leave. It'll only take me an hour at the most to send him back to his wife, all weepy and ashamed I let him steal a feel upstairs. I mean to play him on the line like a lovesick suckerfish and reel him in after seeing you safely on your way up to Denver, see?"

The Fargo Kid commenced to unbutton his shirt as she rejoined him on the bed, but he sounded pissed as he observed, "You really must have felt deprived in that Iowa State Woman's Penitentiary. Is the son of a bitch as good-looking as me, Creasy?"

She began to unbutton his fly for him as she explained, "When I'm in the mood I don't much care what a man might *look* like as long as he knows how to *do* me right. But if it's any comfort to you, I don't mean to shack up with a lawman down this way without good cause. I want it distinctly understood I was a hundred miles from the scene of the crime when you pay Longarm back for my poor brother!"

As she pulled off his boots, the Fargo Kid frowned up at her to state, "I'm missing something, here. Didn't you tell me last night, as we were chatting dog style, you'd sent a letter from K.C. warning that federal man you were fixing to kill him?"

As she hauled off his pants she demurely replied, "Just as I sent that message from you, postmarked a couple of railroad stops away. For the same tactical reasons, kid. We want Longarm watching out for *me* as *you* move in on *him*. Meanwhile, your own enemies down *this* way will be on guard agaist *you*, not a loose-living slut shacked up with a county deputy. Haven't you ever shot ducks from a blind, for Pete's sake?"

He grinned wolfishly as she tossed his pants aside and flopped on the bed beside him and once again he managed not to make that remark the midget made about the naked fat lady in that dirty pool hall joke. As the small but well endowed Fargo Kid entered his companion in crime the old-fashioned way, he chortled, "I follow your drift. The ones I'd like to see dead won't have a chance against anybody sneaky and soft looking as you, whilst I ought to be able to walk right up to this Longarm and just whip my old pissoliver out and . . ."

"Don't even think of slapping leather on the one and original Custis Long!" She wrapped her powerful legs around him as she bit down with her innards for emphasis and warned, "My brother, Cotton, could have taken you on along with John Wesley Hardin and both the Thompson brothers, and Longarm would probably *still* have beaten poor Cotton to the draw! I strongly advise you back-shoot him. But first you'll want to cut him out of the herd so's nobody sees you doing it. Once you kill a lawman, it can be a bother getting away, unless, of course, the law is looking for somebody that doesn't look a thing like you!"

The Fargo Kid began moving in her the way he knew she liked it as he marveled, "Do Jesus if you don't plan ahead for such an impulsive screwer, Creasy! Thanks to them letters you sent, Mel Stuart, Crimp Gooding and that false-hearted Trixie will die thinking they've been killed by me whilst Longarm will die thinking he's being killed by *you*. But hold on, if everyone else knows you were down this way when Longarm was shot . . ."

"They won't be able to charge me with shit!" she demurely replied, moving massively under him as she purred, "Unlike yourself, I'm not on the run from anybody. Thanks to my prison release papers and an ironclad alibi, I'll be free to deny I ever sent any fool letters and be on my merry way. If I were you, I'd head for Canada. You'd have a time passing yourself off as a Mex."

He paused in midstroke to thoughtfully ask, "You mean, once we part company here in Pueblo we'll get to . . . do like so no more?"

23

She sighed. "Oh, shit, don't stop *now*, you silly! We've at least until Tuesday night before it will be safe for you to make a break from here. But I'll tell you what. If you still want to get together with me, like so, we can work out some safe place to meet again, once things cool off, both here and up Denver way."

He kissed her wetly, stretching some, and said they had a deal. Then he was glad she had those long legs wrapped around his waist. Because she'd have bucked him out and off for certain as she bumped and ground with considerable passion, treating him to one of the most prolonged ejaculations he could recall as she literally sucked on his throbbing erection with her quivering insides.

But as sanity returned while they shared another smoke atop the rumpled sweat-soaked bedding, the Fargo Kid asked, "How do you mean to go after Crimp Gooding and them others, here in Pueblo, with one of the county deputies enjoying such favors from you, Creasy?"

She calmly replied, "I won't have to worry about that before I read in the papers how I avenged my poor unfortunate brother in the company of a lawman a hundred miles away. Thanks to that death threat I sent to Longarm, they'll search high and low for me, not you, until they find me here with an ironclad alibi. I mean to make sure Roy Manx brags about his conquest to his pals because I just can't trust any man whose wife can't trust him. Wouldn't it be fun if I could get one or more other deputies mooning about after my fair white body?"

The Fargo Kid grimaced and remarked, "Lord knows you could take it like a soldier, you horny thing. But are you saying you don't mean to go after Will, Crimp or Trixie *before* I kill that Longarm for you? You sure expect one hell of a credit line from a pal risking his ass for you, Creasy!"

She purred, "If it wasn't for me you'd have no ass to

risk, come Monday morning, kid. Do you hear me saying *I* don't trust *you*?"

To which he could only reply, "I surely do. You just said I have to kill Longarm for you before you even try for one of my targets! Were you expecting me to double-cross you by just going on past the Colorado line without even frowning at a lawman with Longarm's rep?"

"The thought never crossed my mind," she lied, reaching down between the two of them to fondle the only thing big about him as she explained, "If only you'd pay attention, I'll lay out the plan once again. Once the letter I sent here to Pueblo arrives, your false friends and the local law are going to be on guard and on the prod for days, but, meanwhile, I'll be sharing pillow talk with at least one of the very lawmen guarding against you. They'll search for you here, and they'll search for you yonder whilst, meanwhile, other lawmen up Denver way will be on the prod for *me*, not a sweet little boy like you, no offense. Your job will be easier. You only have to hit one target to satisfy my soul and be on your way, with nobody suspecting a natural man of modest size and appearance instead of a spectacular freak like me."

He said, "Aw, honey-bunch, you ain't no freak. I think you're right purdy!"

She said, "Pay attention. I know what I look like. Longarm and his pals will be watching for somebody who looks like me. By the time I read his obit in the *Post* or *Rocky Mountain News*, they'll have heard someone answering to such a description was down this way all the while, trying to go straight in the arms of the law. Once I'm free and clear, not before, I'll be free to discreetly pick off your ex-lover gal and those two pards who turned you in for the bounty. I'm sort of looking forward to cutting the treacherous throat of your Trixie. What tricks might she have that I don't have?"

"I can't think of any," he honestly replied; adding, "I

ain't sure I fancy the notion of Will and Crimp living so much longer than your Custis Long, though!"

She purred, "I forget who said revenge was a dish that tasted best served cold. You've got to learn patience if you mean to enjoy such finer tastes with me, kid. Pay attention, damn it! Once I've been accused and cleared of Longarm's murder, nobody is ever going to suspect me of killing three people I have never been known to be on good or bad terms with! Before you ask what's to prevent me from double-crossing *you* by neglecting my own chores down this way after you've killed Longarm for me, use your head as well as your pecker for a fucking minute! You *know* too much for me to double-cross you. You know I was the one who just busted you out of jail, and you have three killings on me already. So what's three more, before I'll be free to start over with a clean slate, with my brother avenged and a prison release to wave in their dumb faces?"

He decided, "When you put things that way, I reckon we got to hang together as pals or hang seperate as double-crossers. Where did you say we might meet up again, once all this sneaky shit is over and done with?"

Then he hissed, "Ooh, sheeesss!" as she rolled atop him to impale her massive torso on his semierection.

It hardly stayed semierect as the gigantic Increase Younger got to moving atop him with her pendulous tits slapping him back and forth across the face whilst she soothed, "Satisfy me good so's I'll be able to prick-tease that deputy when he comes back for sweet stuff this evening. We'll have plenty of time to work out a place to meet later. You won't be leaving for days, and I'm so glad!"

He said that made two of them as he secretly plotted to finish the job right by doing her in, too, once she'd killed Will, Trixie and Crimp. For then *his* score would

26

be settled, and he'd have no call to leave a single person alive to tell the tale.

He had no way of knowing—how could he have?—that even as she was enjoying all he had to offer to the hilt, the bodacious Increase Younger was planning to meet up with him indeed, for a last and final settlement of her blood feud with Custis Long.

She'd been hoping he'd suggest, himself, they meet somewhere again as soon as everyone the two of them were after had been killed. So far the deadly little killer had behaved as predictably as a windup toy. Increase Younger liked that in a man.

Chapter 4

Meanwhile, far to the north, it had taken Longarm and Alvina Witherspoon a tad longer to wind up in bed together but once they had, they'd enjoyed one another even more because neither had been planning to murder the other.

If Longarm enjoyed a rep for a certain smoothness with the unfair sex, it was simply because he'd learned at an early age that few men born of mortal woman had ever really seduced a woman. They just liked to say you'd seduced them after they'd seduced you. For whilst it only took a man a glance to decide whether he wanted to lay a woman or not, with few if any women getting left out, women took as long as fifteen minutes deciding whether they wanted to lay a man or not, and many a man had blown his chances in those first all important opening moves. But unless he did or said something to change her mind before she'd made it up, he only had to resolve to take his beating like a man at a time and place of her choosing.

If a woman didn't fancy you, there was simply no way short of forceable rape or a commercial transaction you were ever going to ring her chimes. If she *did* fancy you, flowers, books, candy or the walking of picket fences were optional as long as you didn't blow it as you both pretended it was your own horny notion.

Since Longarm had long since learned to follow the lady's lead in such matters, Alvina naturally shed a sheepish tear and allowed she should have listened to those warnings about Denver's answer to Don Juan, once he'd made her come a couple of times and suggested they share a smoke and get their second winds before they did it again.

Alvina naturally waited until he'd fumbled a three-for-a-nickel and a light from his duds on the rug and had them both smoking friendly, propped up on pillows against the head of her four poster with one of her naked legs draped over his bare knee before she softly sobbed and murmured, "I can't believe I'm really smoking a cigar, stark naked, in bed with a man I barely know in broad daylight!"

Longarm placed the pencil-thin smoke to her pouty lips as he soothed, "This ain't a cigar, it's a *cheroot*, and I won't peek at your privates if you don't peek at mine, honey lamb. As for barely knowing me, I thought you said you'd been reading about me in the papers long before I first came in for some cough syrup that time."

She exhaled a heap of smoke for such a daintly looking thing and snuggled closer as she confided, "You never told me at the time you wanted that medicine for the cough of that sickly bootblack down on the corner. It's a good thing you came back for more, once I found out you'd put him up in a hotel room and hired that cleaning woman to sit with him. What ever happened to that boy, by the way? I haven't seen him around this neighborhood of late, Custis."

Longarm took a drag on the cheroot to buy some time for choosing words before he casually replied, "I arranged to have that orphan asylum out Arvada way take him in

30

until he's old enough to blacken boots when it ain't snow-ing a mile above sea level for Pete's sake."

He'd been braced for it. But it appeared Alvina hadn't heard of his warm friendship with Miss Morgana Floyd, the head matron of the orphan asylum in question. Lord willing and the creeks didn't rise, old Morgana might never hear of old Alvina.

He saw he'd led Alvina's she-male line of questioning clear of his pull with the orphan asylum when she asked how such a sickly young boy had wound up blackening boots on the streets of Denver.

He shrugged his bare shoulders to reply, "There's a lot of that going around. Folk back east with kids as well as the consumption hear the weather out this way might cure their lungs. So they head west with their hopes and their kids, and when they die the kids wind up on their own, a long ways from any other kith or kin. That sickly boot-black who sort of introduced us, Lord love him, says he aims to be a lawman when he grows up, if they won't have him over to the fire department."

Alvina said, "I can see why. You're not half as mean as those newspaper stories make you out, Custis. I'll bet you had a perfectly good reason for shooting that Cotton Younger, didn't you?"

Longarm blew a thoughtful smoke ring and decided, "Had no other choice. He was fixing to shoot me. I was trying to arrest him, nice, over to Salt Lake City, when he went for his own gun, and after that things tend to blur. You'd never know this, reading Ned Buntline's dime novels, but gunfights are seldom planned ahead in detail, down to crossing every *t* and dotting every *i*."

He thought some and decided, "The Salt Lake papers got the details a tad dramatic, and the story got turned into a sort of fairy-tale as other papers picked it up and passed it on with added local color. I don't recall swap-ping lead with Cotton Younger up and down a marble

31

staircase. Our fight was more confusing but less colorful as all that. Like I said, I tried to arrest him in a second-story courtroom, where he'd been pretending to be somebody innocent. A fight broke out betwixt two women involved in the case, and I couldn't fire back with them betwixt us as the big moose made a break for it. I had to fire from a prone position once I'd chased him out in the hall and ducked the lead he was throwing my way. I gut-shot him in the hallway. He tried for or fell down the stairwell to end up dead on a landing. I can see by your glazed expression you like the newspaper version a lot better. I sometimes remember things that way my ownself. Real life can be so tedious next to shorthand notes."

She sighed. "That outlaw's sister you told me about must have read the simpler newspaper version in her prison cell. But where does any version have you taking unfair advantage of a wanted outlaw, dear?"

He grimaced and replied, "Riders of the owlhoot trail, along with their kith and kin, seem to feel it's *always* unfair when a lawman is the survivor.

"You have to buy that Hindu *Kama Sutra* and other naughty books in plain wrappers from under the counter. But they'll allow an impressionable schoolboy named Frank or Jesse to check out a copy of *Robin Hood* from most any school library, and any lawman can tell you that's about the dirtiest book ever written."

Alvina laughed and mockingly accused, "You've peeked at the *Kama Sutra*, too? Where in *Robin Hood* does it suggest Robin and his Maid Marian got . . . you know, down and dirty?"

Longarm easily replied, "Robin plays dirty from Chapter One. He's poaching game in a hunting preserve with the game wardens and the county sheriff described as the villains. The story goes downhill from there as a self-described bandit recruits a gang of outlaws to rob innocent travelers passing through a wooded stretch along a public right of way."

"They robbed from the rich to help the poor," she objected.

Longarm snorted, "Of couse they robbed from the rich. Outlaws have always robbed from the rich because the poor have no money. The tale of Robin Hood and his merry men has them gloating and joshing as they rob everbody from armored knights to unarmed monks and preachers and, before you say word one about the Reformation or the evils of the unholy inquisition, neither Robin Hood nor a single one of his Merry Men could have been *Protestants* at such an early date. There was only one church. Robin Hood and all his kith and kin belonged to it, and you know what folk think of a skunk who'd rob the poor box or filch from the collection plate in his own church!"

Alvina asked what Robin Hood's religion had to do with the elder sister of the late Cotton Younger.

He said, "Like her kid brother and a heap of other modern outlaws, she's doubtless sold herself the notion that anything goes as long as it's against the law, because all folk who obey or uphold the law were created the legitimate prey of the merry riders of the owlhoot trail. To Increase Younger, her brother had every right to gun *me*, whilst I sinned against her and all creation when I gunned him instead. I'm sure she's never asked herself what that awful Sheriff of Nottingham used as justification when he persecuted poor innocent Robin on charges of highway robbery, poaching, trespass and most likely occasional rape. To Robin Hood or Increase Younger, the badge I pack is an offense against God and man. So it's lucky for me she's easy to spot at a distance, and Lord knows how I'll ever manage once I do. I hate the way the papers report it when a lawman has to gun a woman!"

"Does that happen often, Custis?" she quietly asked.

He took another drag on their shared cheroot and replied, "Not often. But it happens. The man who first said God created all men and Sam Colt created all men equal left women out of the adage. But two hundred grains of lead from the muzzle of a woman's .44-40 can kill a man of any size as dead, and they say Increase Younger is big enough to handle a .44-40 or even a ten-gauge."

"I don't think you could shoot a woman," the woman he was in bed with decided, adding, "You like us too much, *this* way, to put two hundred grains of lead in our poor little tumtums!"

Longarm snubbed out the cheroot to free that hand for action as he held her closer, suggesting he was fixing to drill her with yet another weapon. As he began to rock the little man in her canoe she moaned, "Ooh, don't tease me, Custis! Prove to me you've read that naughty *Kama Sutra*! Do it to me really dirty, this time!"

But of course, once he'd rolled her facedown and forked a leg over to mount her in a position midway betwixt Cleopatra on a sofa and dog style, she protested that she didn't want him peeking at her winking rectum by broad daylight, for heaven's sake. So he lowered his naked front to her bare back and wetly chewed one of her ears as she arched her spine to purr, "Oh, Christ! I've never felt a . . . you know, at *that* angle! What do you call that big old nasty thing of yours, Custis?"

He confided, with her earlobe between his grinning teeth, "When we're alone I call it my best friend. Its job description is My Old Organ Grinder."

She moaned, "I can see why! Or should I say I can *feel* why, and it sure grinds fine! Do you like the way my . . . you know, feels?"

He honestly replied, "Can't recall a ring dang doo that's ever felt so swell." For this was the simple truth, at the moment. He had no call to observe that farther down the road of life he'd doubtless feel the same way in other sweet surroundings. For the nicest thing to be said for most any woman, provided one didn't overdo it with any particular woman, was the feeling as one moved in and out of almost any woman that there'd never been a nicer piece of ass on God's green earth since Adam and Eve had torn off that first swell piece back in that garden of Eden.

When a man *studied* on it, usually about the time he was trying to come the fourth or fifth time, he was inclined to compare the pussy he was in at the moment with pussies of the past, or mayhaps from his less possible daydreams. But Mother Nature or Professor Darwin over to London town had designed mankind to sincerely cotton to the romantic here-and-now, lest they slow down and lose the beat before the big climax of the piece.

But since they'd climaxed earlier and Longarm was a considerate lover who could sense when a gal was due for a change of pace, he slid them both across the rumpled bedding to where he could plant his bare feet on the rug and haul her shapely petite derriere high as his own hips to thrust in and out faster with a good grip on her own hip bones.

As he did so, Alvina sobbed, "Oh, no! Are you peeking at my . . . you know, you horrid man?"

He said, "*Asshole* is the word you were groping for, and I must say I purely admire your asshole, Miss Alvina. Don't try to tuck it under like that. You got to arch your spine the other way if you expect me to hit bottom from this position, see?"

She moaned, "My God, you are hitting bottom, and it hurts so good! Have you ever shoved that . . . organ grinder up a lady's . . . *asshole,* Custis?"

He almost said, "Hasn't everybody?" but decided it sounded a tad more delicate to reply, "I have it on good authority that most gals find it painful, whilst the few who

35

seem to fancy it are inclined to come down with delicate medical conditions."

She giggled, her face buried in a pillow as she confided, "You mean they develope piles and spastic colons. You forget I sell medical supplies when I'm not behaving like a depraved slut on the Sabbath. But I confess I've often wondered what it might be like, just once, to, you know, take it in the ass?"

He said, "That's as delicate a way as it might be put. Don't you want to finish coming, this way, first?"

She said, "Ooh, yesss! How did we wind up talking about it instead of *doing* it, darling?"

"We must be due for a longer rest and mayhaps some coffee and cake, I reckon." He decided as he proceeded to concentrate in the business at hand, pounding harder until she came. Longarm was at that stage when a man begins to wonder what he'd ever found so attractive about the shapely naked rump he was so hard at work with. So *he* faked it and fell across the bed beside her, knowing why Mother Nature had provided for *that* feeling as well, lest her poor critters never stop until they'd screwed their fool selves to death.

As he'd foreseen, when Alvina recovered her breath, she seemed more interested in other appetites, now that she'd satisfied her old ring dang doo. Longarm felt too spent and content to do anything but loll there, smiling up fondly as his gracious hostess whipped them up a pot of coffee and half a store-bought marble cake to share in bed together.

As they nibbled and sipped side by side, innocent as naked kids by a swimming hole for the moment, Alvina said she had to open her shop come Monday morn, but allowed he'd be welcome to stay holed up there in her quarters until the danger from Iowa State blew over. It was a caution how folk wanted to take care of you once you'd taken care of them.

But Longarm was forced to wistfully reply, "Ain't paid to hide out from outlaws, more's the pity. They pay me to hunt outlaws down, and we've just agreed this would be just about the last place in town I'd be likely to meet up with Increase Younger."

She pleaded, "You don't mean to just . . . eat and run, do you?"

He set a slice of cake aside to pat her naked hip and assure her she was stuck with him until Monday morn.

She asked what happened them.

He honestly replied, "Can't say. Like my boss told me, I get crank letters all the time. If she wasn't bluffing she's had time enough to circle in on me more than once by this time."

Chapter 5

Longarm was still thinking about that when he showed up for work Monday morn. Seated across a cluttered desk from his boss, back in the oak-paneled inner sanctum of U.S. Marshal William Vail, Longarm said, "Half the outlaws I run in assure in the heat of the moment that they mean to clean my plow the day they get out of prison. But it's a caution how they seem to cool down once they find themselves outside the bars, free to go get screwed, blewed and tattooed or come looking for a rematch with a gent who's already gotten the drop on 'em on a gloomier occasion.

"That big old sister of Cotton Younger may have meant it when she sent that first death threat in the first enthusiasm of freedom. She may have still been dallying with the notion as she drifted west some more. But getting arrested up yonder in Jimtown, just for standing out in a crowd of whores, might well have persuaded her there are better ways to spend one's remaining years than back in prison or worse. What if all this time we've been stewing about her that big old bawd's gone on out to the Great Basin or even the West Coast? A six-foot-six anything with any looks could find a heap of action along the Bar-

bary Coast, now that the stock market crash of '72 is no more than a bitter memory."

The older lawman shook his head to reply, "What if the dog hadn't stopped to shit, and the rabbit hadn't got away? I play cards regular with the local police commissioner. So Denver P.D. has been keeping an eye on the Union Station and the Overland Terminal down to Tremont Place. But after that there are simply too many routes a gal could come in by, sidesaddle or dressed as a man astride a cow pony. Calamity Jane Canary gets away with passing her fool self off as a man on occasion, and she ain't near as tall in the saddle as our Miss Increase Younger!"

Longarm grimaced and said, "You sure paint a rosy picture, boss. Next thing I know you'll have me slapping leather on some tall but otherwise innocent cowboy asking directions to the Parthenon Saloon!"

Billy Vail nodded soberly and said, "Too many ways she could come at you in a crowd. Got a chore that'll take you off the streets of Denver, and out on open range where you can size up anyone headed your way before they're within rifle range."

He rummaged through the papers on his cluttered desk to find what he was looking for as he said, "Summons from the Land Office. Nester waved a shotgun at the Department of the Interior when they tried to serve it. Land Management suggested, and Judge Dickerson down the hall agrees, it might be best to serve the sons of bitches more formal with a court order delivered by this office in the person of yourself. It ain't all that far, and the immigrant has had time to consider what a dumb position he's taken by this time."

As Vail handed the court order across the desk to Longarm he thought he had to add, "You'll see an extra day's pay, come the end of the month, if you have to arrest him and manage to bring him in *alive* for a change!"

Longarm put the summons away without comment. They'd told him the first day on the job he got four bits for serving legal papers, two dollars a head plus transportation expenses for making arrests and not one red cent if he had to *kill* a want. It hardly seemed fair until one reflected on how tempting it might be to just gun the son of a bitch and save oneself the bother of bringing him back alive. That pesky Cotton Younger out Utah way had left Longarm out of pocket for all those miles he might have billed the Justice Department for, at six cents a mile going out and ten cents a mile coming back from Salt Lake City with the rascal. So he felt no call to assure Billy Vail he wasn't fixing to gun a nester over a disputed homestead claim.

Despite books such as *Black Beauty*, practical working men in an age of steam and horsepower seldom owned their own mounts. Longarm naturally kept his own saddle and trail-gear handy for those occasions Billy Vail sent him out in the field. But seeing the summons he'd be serving on one T.S. Jensen was only an hour's ride out along the Overland Trace to the northeast, Longarm simply hired a stock saddle to go with the bay livery nag, an older but still serviceable cavalry brute the livery had saved from the dogfood knacker by bidding a dollar more at that Remount Service auction. The stable hand told Longarm her name was Siwash and warned she balked at railroad tracks or cattle guards.

Since he meant to cross neither that morning, Longarm simply rode northeast through first fashionable and then increasingly haphazard surroundings until he passed a last hog farm for a spell to trot old Siwash downslope and walk her upslope across gently rolling short-grass prairie, punctuated by clumps of "soapweed," as yucca was called on the northern ranges.

The soapweed was way greener than the grass, this far into summer, albeit the buffalo, bunch and grama grass

41

still had some growing left in it, closer to the roots. The way grass grew, like human hair you could trim away or feed to cows, accounted for the current golden age of the western beef industry. As long as stockmen grazed their cows sensibly and left the damned roots in place, grass grew back, lush as ever, spring greenup after greenup.

It took an entire asshole to bust up the high plains of Colorado with a fucking plow unless he had the ways and means to irrigate his exposed prairie loam under a sky that offered ten inches of rain or less a year, west of say longitude 100°.

As he rode Siwash up a long grade at a walk, Longarm found himself singing the familiar

> "I ain't made a dollar, I ain't made a cent.
> All of the grubstake I had has been spent.
> Our cow has gone dry and my pony's gone lame,
> And I'm starving to death on my government claim!"

Siwash didn't laugh. It wasn't all that funny a song. Honest Abe and his Congress of '62 had meant well and, farther east, a quarter section, or 160 acres, made a swell farm. Twice the average size of those swell Penn State farms so famous for their butter, eggs and shoofly pies. But dry farming out *this* way was a sometimes thing and whilst the greenup had been fair that year, the summer before had been one dusty bastard. So a show-cause from the land office was doubtless easier to raise than anything else out here along the Overland Trace.

They called it that because such roadbed as was there consisted of the wheel ruts of the Overland stagecoach that still ran from Denver up to Julesburg near the Nebraska Line. Billy Vail had only sent him an easy five miles out that way, however, and as he spotted the daisy head of an Aermotor Brand windmill over the rise ahead he figured that had to be the Jensen place, out in the middle of nowhere and inhabited by greenhorns and grasshoppers!

As he rode in, he idly wondered whether the Jensen kids played with the big gray lubber grasshoppers out this way. Most kids did. There was a children's book out, advising kids how to fashion paper boats and sleds for bugs to pull or ride in. The author assured his young readers it was easy to make a cage for a ferocious spider or grasshopper by slicing two round sections of cork, or a carrot, and then driving a bunch of Momma's straight pins through the top slice and into the bottom to form the circular cage of real steel bars.

It didn't say what Momma would have to say about all this, or why in thunder anyone wanted to keep a bug in a cage to begin with. But Longarm had been a kid one time, and he suspected that in his day he might have tried to make such a cage for, say, a black widow, at least.

He knew why he was thinking about kids. Hardly any single gent who spoke English seemed to file a homestead claim at this late date. The word about raising more dust than barley out this way had gotten about east of Omaha. But the better bottomlands, where the rains came down more often, had been claimed early on, with Scandinavian folk named Jensen and such doing better in places like Minnesota or Wisconsin. So the Jensens ahead were likely second-generation nesters or new nesters entire. He knew that in either case they figured to have big-eyed kids who'd have a tough time grasping why their dear old dad was apparently at war with the federal government of these United States.

Topping a rise, he had a better view of the Jensen homestead ahead. Somebody had put forth a heartbreaking amount of sweat and toil in trying to prove his claim.

The way the Homestead Act of '62 worked, as intended

to settle the empty federal lands of the west, one family head was entitled to lay claim to the quarter section of his choice for a modest filing fee. He had to prove his claim by "improving" the raw land and occupying it more than six months of every year for five whole years before the land was his to sell, borrow against, or lose in a game of chance. Since the land office wanted a serious discussion with farmer Jensen about the claim ahead, Longarm likely figured Jensen had done something wrong.

Riding in at a walk, Longarm was unable to make out what all the fuss might be about. He knew lawyers sent their kids through college arguing just what constituted an "improvement." But stringing all that Glidden wire had to count for something. They'd fenced the property once around and divided it into four forty-acre plots with more of the same. A mile around and two quarter miles cross-ways took many a costly reel of galvanized barbwire.

That fancy windmill made in Chicago had cost like fire as well, albeit there was no way in hell to draw water with that old oaken bucket of song this far from the flood-plains of the South Platte. That wind-powered tube-well was doubtless drawing from at least fifty feet down at this time of the year.

He could see their southeast forty acres had been planted to barley, stirrup high and commencing to set seed for early autumn, if anybody named Jensen was still out this way to harvest it. So some old-timer had told Jensen about the market for barley-malt over to that big brewery in the foothills of the Front Range.

The fair-sized sod house faced southeast to catch the morning sun over high and lower rooftops of sod-walled stable and barn. They'd built a pole corral and drilled in cottonwood shoots to form an inverted V-shaped wind-break aimed due north, weather and grasshoppers permit-ting, in say five or six more years. As they approached the gap in the perimeter wire secured by a cattle-guard,

Longarm told his livery mount, "I can see why our excitable Swede got excited when the land office tried to serve him with a summons, Siwash. The poor bastard must have slaved like a beaver on black coffee out this way, along with his wife and kids, alas."

Having been warned by that stable hand, Longarm didn't try to walk the bay mare across the cattle-guard. He reined in to dismount and lead her, soothingly assuring her, "I know it seems as if I'm out to bust all four of your legs and shoot you, Siwash. But you can do it if only you'll try."

Getting her to try was a bother. Like others of its simple but sort of slick design, the cattle-guard barring entrance or exit on the part of livestock consisted of no more than half a dozen cottonwood logs half buried across the entryway from side to side with a two or three inch gap between them at ground level. A man, a child or a critter who really wanted to could walk across the logs, one to another, with little effort and no danger to life or limb if they missed a high spot to step down between the peeled logs. But all cows and a heap of horses prefered to keep their hooves on sod, or, failing sod, flat bare dirt less confusing to stride across.

A cow driven by hunger, thirst or other desperation *could* cross a cattle-guard. Just as they *could* bust through a barbwire fence once they put their minds to it. Cattle-guards, like barbwire, worked on the simple principle that cows were conservative by nature.

Livery nags, as Siwash proceeded to demonstrate, could be downright stubborn about tiptoeing across splintery sun-silvered logs. So her pragmatic rider suggested, "Have it your way, you poor dumb brute!" as he tethered her to a gatepost, adding, "You just stand here as the sun rises higher whilst I mosey on in for that cool drink in the shade I wasn't able to talk you into!"

Patting the legal papers under his tobacco-tweed frock

coat to have them ready, Longarm walked towards the cluster of sod buildings to the west of the southeast forty and their central gate. Seeing he'd left his own McClellan army saddle at home, and seeing this was a simple serving of a court order, he wasn't walking in with his Winchester '73, and it might have seemed needlessly dramatic to clear the grips of the .44-40 six-gun he wore cross-draw under the tails of his coat. So it seemed likely the folk in the house had him down as unarmed when a sash-window opened near their whitewashed front door and a high-pitched voice called out something hysterical in Swedish.

Longarm didn't break stride but found himself instinctively veering toward the nearby corner of their sod barn as he called back in the same soothing tone he'd just tried on Siwash, "I regret to say I don't speak any Scanda-hoovian dialects. If you can't speak English, might you savvy 'Spañol or mayhaps High Plains sign lingo?"

A more childish voice called out in English, "Ma says she don't want none and you'd better *git*, mister!"

Longarm kept coming as he called back, "I ain't a mister. I'm the law, and your folk have to accept what I've come to deliver whether they want it or not! It ain't for them nor me to decide. I'm packing a federal court order and . . ."

He crabbed to one side, his sentence unfinished as the dulcet song of a repeating rifle rent the air to hide that window and half the soddy in dense white gunsmoke as Longarm drew his own weapon and dropped to the dust to peer 'round the corner like a brownie hiding behind a toadstool.

As the smoke across the way cleared, that same childish voice called out, "You'd better not come no closer, Mr. Lawman! Ma says she'll *aim* Pa's old Henry rifle at you, next time!"

Longarm called back, "I ain't headed nowheres, kid,

46

and neither are any of you-all! Where's your pa if your ma don't speak English?"

The kid called back, "Pa died last winter of an ague. But before he did he made us all promise we'd never give up this land he worked so hard to prove, and Ma says, in Swedish, you'll have to kill us all to take this land away from us, now. We got *bones* buried on this land, Mr. Lawman. Pa and our poor old aunt Greta and a baby brother born dead our first winter out here! Why don't you just go on back to town and leave us alone! We ain't been bothering nobody out this way, and we don't want nobody bothering us. It's as simple as that, see?"

To which Longarm could only reply in a weary tone, "I'm afraid I don't see things that simple, kid. When it comes to the law, things are seldom simple and it's not for you, me nor your Ma to say what the Bureau of Land Management has in mind for this spread!"

Chapter 6

Longarm was pinned down against the sunny south wall of the barn, and the sun got warmer as it rose ever higher in a cloudless cobalt blue sky. He took off his coat and lit a cheroot to smoke as he read over the court order all this fuss was about. He was too far from the gate for old Siwash to hear his words, even if she'd been capable of following his drift as he told her, "I told you you'd be sorry. With you tethered yonder I'd have to break cover dashing back to you, and how would I explain this to Billy Vail if I did run away from one crazy woman with an antiquated Henry?"

He swore sincerely at the Widow Jensen as he perused the show-cause she seemed bound and determined to refuse at gunpoint. Billy Vail had sent him out this way to avoid a gunfight with a woman, and she had at least one kid in yonder with her, bless her greenhorn ways!

The stubborn old mare didn't deserve his concern. But he couldn't help feeling sorrier for Siwash than he felt for himself as they both got hotter and drier. *He* knew what he was doing there, but had he known the two-hour ride was going to turn out so tedious, he'd have brought at least one canteen along and hung on to it. Smoking helped at first. But he passed on a second cheroot once the first one he'd smoked all the way down left his tongue feeling like dry leaves in the pocket of a wool overcoat. He fished out his pocket watch and swore at it when it told him he **had nigh eight hours of sunlight ahead of him before it** might be safe to pussyfoot in or further away.

Which move might churn a man's guts worse was the question before the house. One woman inside that soddy with one repeating rifle would hardly be able to hold him back if he made up his mind to move in on 'em after sundown.

Whilst he made up his mind, he showed the brim of his coffee-brown Stetson around the southwest corner of their barn to let them know he was still there. He didn't want them wondering where else he might be until he moved that way.

With any luck, she'd be trying to hold a bead on his present position in the treacherous light of the gathering dusk. So that would be the time to move north along the back walls of the barn and stable to approach the house around the back poles of that corral to bust in by way of any back door or window handy and . . . then what? She'd be holed up in a dark house if she had a lick of sense, and he had to worry about shooting kids whilst she'd be free to shoot at anybody darkening a door or window. There had to be a better way. The stakes in this game weren't worth so much as a black eye to anybody with one sober spoonful of brains!

Maybe if he just went on back to town, told them he'd seen no way of serving the fool papers without risking innocent blood and let them study on it . . .

"They'll send a corporal's squad from Camp Weld after they finish laughing at such a big sissy!" Longarm muttered aloud with a knowing sigh, adding, "Had Billy Vail wanted the War Department to tend the chore, he'd have requested Camp Weld to take over, and swat my flies if this chore ain't mine, all mine!"

Thanks to the thin air at that altitude, the sweat the sun baked out of him dried fast, without cooling him enough to matter as he and doubtless poor Siwash over yonder got to needing some drinking water, a heap of drinking water, before sundown at the rate the dry heat was mummifying them on the hoof.

Then the whitewashed front door across the barnyard opened and a girl of around ten came out with a picnic basket braced against her skinny young hip by one hand as she waved a white kerchief on a stick with the other, calling out, "Don't shoot me, Mister Lawman, I ain't coming at you with no gun!"

He asked her what else she was packing as she approached in her too big clodhoppers and threadbare blue and pink calico Mother Hubbard. Her honey-blond hair hung down her flat chest in pigtails and her teeth still looked too big for her mouth. But he could see she was fixing to be a looker in a few more years. As he rose to his full considerable height around the corner from her mother's gun sights, she joined him, explaining, "We thought you were likely starting to feel hungry and thirsty out here. Ma said she'd kill you if you came any closer, but it was still her duty as a good Christian to send this basket out to you."

Longarm nodded soberly and said, "I got my own duties, too, but I tick my hat brim to a lady of quality, even though she's *loco en la cabeza*. I'm more thirsty than hungry, and you likely know a horse needs more, more often, than any man or even a mule. Do you reckon your Christian mother would abide your taking a pail of water out to that poor nag tethered to your gate post, Miss . . . ah?"

"Jensen, Pia Jensen," she replied with a toothy smile as she gave him the basket and added, "Wouldn't it be easier to just lead that poor lathered pony into our stable for some water, fodder and above all some shade?"

Longarm said, "She don't want to step over your cattle-guard, Miss Pia. That's how come I left her out there to bake as she contemplates the error of her ways."

The Swedish or Swedish-American girl said she felt sure she could lead a horse to water this late in the afternoon. So he told her to go for it as he hunkered down with the basket to find ham and cheese on rye sandwiches and a jug of what surely smelled and tasted like plain water. It was tepid and likely too hard to do laundry with. It tasted refreshing as iced lager going down.

He hadn't started on the sandwiches when Pia came back, leading old Siwash by the reins as if they were old pals. The sassy kid grinned at him to say, "See? I told you so! Aren't you going to eat those sandwiches, Mr. Lawman? I made 'em, myself."

It wouldn't have been polite to tell a young lady he had reservations against biting into anything tasty and pungent enough to hide all sorts of nasty surprises he could think of. So he just said, "Later tonight, seeing your mother means to force my hand. I doubt she'd believe us if we tried to tell her how these papers she refuses to accept might translate into Swedish."

It worked. The kid asked him what the land grabbing rascals were accusing her poor widowed mother of, just to steal the homestead poor Pa had worked himself to death to prove.

Longarm said, "If the two of you believe the federal government is out to grab land from anyone but Mr. Lo, the poor Indian, nothing I can say or show you in black and white on paper is going to do you a lick of good. I met this missionary gal one time who told me they'd warned her not to waste time on the invincibly stupid savages in this world so filled with brighter savages who needed saving. Anyone can see the U.S. Congress passed the Homestead Act of 1862 just to settle white folk on land already owned by the federal government because they wanted an excuse to steal the land from somebody. Federal open range the government already owns needs to be stolen out from under potential taxpayers before they qualify to pay taxes on it. Anybody can see *that*."

She hesitated as Siwash fought the reins some, now that she was in off the open range and recalling how stables and water seemed to be associated in her less clear view of the situation. Pia jerked the bit to make Siwash behave as she asked what those rogues from the land office *did* want if they didn't want to *victim* her Ma.

Longarm said, "*Eviction* is the word you were after, Miss Pia. The papers the land office has been trying to serve you-all with ain't an eviction notice, albeit at the rate she's going I wouldn't bet on your mother holding out much longer against the U.S. of A. I know they didn't teach this in Swedish schools, Miss Pia, but a few years ago a whole mess of southern states, with their own army and navy, tried to stand off the U.S. of A. and it didn't work."

He let that sink in and bent over to pick up the court order and original summons as he explained, "A federal judge has ordered your mother to answer this summons from the land office. The summons gives her ten days from her acceptance of the same to appear before them and show cause, or answer questions, as you might say it in Swedish."

"What kind of questions?" she demanded, suspiciously.

He said, "Ain't sure, but now that you've told me your Pa died out here to be buried on his own land, unofficious, I suspect the land office wants to be brung up-to-date on that. Your homestead claim would be in his name, not hers. Did they send some form out for him to fill out in English? If She never answered it in any lingo, it could cause all sorts of confusion as they shuffled papers back in town."

Pia gasped, "Oh, I think we *did* get a letter from Denver earlier this year. Ma said we didn't know anybody she wanted to talk to who couldn't speak, read or write Swedish. Do you think the land office might have sent it?"

Longarm said, "Can't see who else might have, seeing your folk had no Swedish pals in Denver. The Bureau of Land Management rides homesteaders with a gentle hand on the reins, knowing they have more than enough to discourage 'em and not wanting 'em discouraged. But from time to time, say once every year or so, they do like to check and see if anybody's still proving a claim."

He let her digest that, then suggested, "Why don't we find out the easy way, Miss Pia? This summons gives your Pa in point of fact, or your Ma as a practical matter, ten days to show cause why this family claim should remain in the name of Jensen. Your Ma won't have to say a word to anybody if she's shy about her English. That's what lawyers are for. I know a lady lawyer in Denver I could ask to take your case pro bono, or on the cuff, until such time as you sell that barley this fall. She's called Portia Parkhurst, Esquire, dumb as that sounds, and she loves to stand up for women in court because she feels so . . . womanly. Why don't you take this poor mare on in and have a word with your Ma about what I just said?"

Pia asked, "What if she doesn't believe you? She says when she first got off the boat some Yankee rascal took cruel advantage of her."

Longarm shrugged and said, "In that case, we'll have to do things the hard way. I'll have to arrest her for refusing to obey a court order. When she pays the fine or serves her sentence you may still have this claim to come back to, or the land office may decide some nester more inclined to co-operate with 'em might as well take over, improvements and all. I've seen that happen, Miss Pia.

Pencil-pushing government clerks are inclined to take the path of least resistance. So why don't we see if we can convince your mother she's acting more like a muley Lakota than a sensible Pueblo and see if we can't save your farm?"

The pretty little ragged-ass thing led Siwash on to the stable, and then he saw her vanish into the soddy for a spell as the overhead sun got no cooler and he'd soon polished off all the water.

A thirsty man who ate ham and cheese on rye under an afternoon sun on the high plains was a man who didn't deserve to be running free off a leash.

So he was commencing to feel hungry as well as thirsty when little Pia Jensen came back without her white flag to say he could come on in for a parley if he left his six-gun rig draped over the hitchrail out front. So Longarm agreed, picked up his folded frock coat and followed her in to do as she said. She hadn't said anything about the double derringer attached to the end of his watch chain in his opposing vest pocket.

It felt ten degrees cooler inside the sod house under the thick low pitched roof planted to buffalo grass. There were two smaller children staring big eyed at him from one corner of the combined kitchen and parlor. The Widow Jensen was an older and plainer edition of her daughter, Pia. Homesteading on the high plains was rough on a woman's looks betwixt the hard work and uncertain winds that blew hot and cold but most often bone dry. She sat him at a deal table to serve him coffee and cake whether he'd et those sandwiches or not. So despite her limited grasp of English, she'd Americanized enough to know a house-proud nesting woman was expected to serve coffee and cake to passing riders. He knew without asking nosey questions they were doing better than some on their government claim. So she and the kids were man-

55

aging to carry on the sensible enough dry farming of her late hard-working husband.

With Pia translating, the Widow Jensen demanded to know what *loco en la cabeza* meant and why he'd accused her of acting like a Sioux. Swedish folk had never forgiven the eastern Lakota or Nakota for the Great Sioux uprising back in Minnesota and would always think of them as Sioux, or *treacherous snakes* as the Ojibwa name for Lakota translated.

Pia her daughter he told her, "My border Mex description of your state of mind may have been harsh. Since you see me sitting here at your table, enjoying this swell chocolate cake, you can't be totally crazy in the head. But as for your trying to hold your claim with a gun instead of a lawyer, allow me to tell you the tale of two Indian nations."

He spoke slowly so Pia could translate a sentence at a time as he explained, "Down New Mexico way, you'll find this town called Taos. It's the oldest inhabited township in these United States. Being built by Tanoan speaking Pueblo folk long before Mr. Columbus made that wrong turn to India. *Pueblo* is a Spanish word for folk who live in villages. So it applies to different nations speaking different tongues but holding much the same views as to land tenure. So they understood our kind and our kind understood them when the U.S. of A. took New Mexico away from Old Mexico. Instead of waving guns around, they hired Mex lawyers to petition the land office for title to their ancestral lands and they *got* 'em. But we all know how the *Lakota* made out."

In case they didn't, he continued, "It was a case of a fair price as set under the laws of eminent domain for the Paha Supa, or Black Hills, they'd taken away from other Indians back in the 1700s. Any lawyer worth his salt could have wrangled them more than the government was offering. But they held out for more, and when they didn't get it they went on the warpath and now they're on the run up Canada way and they never got beans for their Paha Supa. So why don't you let me see if I can get a good lady lawyer to stand up to the land office for you, ma'am? It's likely they only want answers to some natural questions, and it surely won't cost you as dear as a gunfight you simply can't win!"

So in the end, the Jensens agreed and Longarm headed back to town full of coffee and cake as he mulled over how he meant to present a pro bono case to Portia Parkhurst, Esquire.

It was likely to cost him a fancy dinner at Romano's, but once she let her graying hair down, old Portia screwed like a mink in heat. What the hell; he just *had* to save that old homestead, didn't he?

Chapter 7

Once Portia had given Longarm a hard time about that bubbly blond stenographer at the federal building, and been truthfully assured he'd never spent a night at home with a gal who prefered after-hours quickies in that file room down the hall, the severely beautiful attorney-at-law said she'd take the case *pro bono* because she couldn't wait to see what that Swedish widow had to offer a man that she didn't.

As they were discussing the matter over a sit-down supper with bread sticks and a candle stuck in a Chianti bottle betwixt them to soften old Portia's jawline a mite, Increase Younger had already hauled County Deputy Roy Manx into bed with her, upstairs, whilst, down in that secret room, the Fargo Kid kept hoping against hope she only meant to string the lawman along up yonder to find out how they were doing.

The two-faced Increase had gotten the show on the road early for the simple reason that she knew a married man would be anxious to get on home to his wife and kids after some slap and tickle on the side and a hard day's work. Increase had chosen a married man to extend her web to the sheriff's department because she'd known Roy Manx would leave her free to move about in the dark of night after bragging about his conquest to other lawmen.

Hoping to encourage his bragging, and not wanting to arouse the suspicions of her other lover, or victim, downstairs, Increase gave Roy Manx one hell of a ride and threw in a French lesson that had him pleading for mercy before she sent him home in time for his supper, walking sort of funny.

Down in their secret love nest, after a hasty whore bath and a vinegar douche, Increase told the worried Fargo Kid, as they were going dog style, "That letter you sent your old pal, Crimp Gooding, stirred things up better than I'd hoped. He ran with it to the law, and, last Deputy Manx heard, old Crimp's still running and so Trixie Davis is alone at that livery and stud set-up they bought with the reward money posted on yourself, you valuable little darling."

The Fargo Kid thrust hard and deep, growling, "I reckon I grew big enough where it matters, and I owe the rest to Mr. Samuel Colt. Did that lawman say anything about Mel Stuart as he was doing this to you upstairs just now?"

Arching her spine to thrust her massive behind up to him, the natural blond with auburn hair on her head these days assured the smaller man, "You have my word as a discriminating slut that Deputy Manx has yet to do me dog style. He said Mel Stuart's holed up at the riding and breeding spread with your loose-living Trixie and a tense expression, guarded for the moment by a brace of county deputies."

As she gyrated her tailbone to wring his throbbing manhood like a dish rag, she demurely continued, "Deputy Manx says they're not too worried about you killing Mel and Trixie. They just want you back to kick the shit out of you before they hang you high. You have them as stirred up as a stomped-on anthill, you ferocious kid. Aside from sending a posse down the line to surround the town of Avondale, the sheriff has another posse chasing Crimp Gooding up the Arkansas into the Front Range and, I almost forgot, he's put out an all-points for you on the Western Union's cross country web. So, in sum, we've got them looking for you just about every fool place you ain't. Roy Manx says they don't see how you could be hiding out here in Pueblo. They figure you're skulking like an Arapaho Red Sash, out and about on the open plains in such fair weather. But ain't it a caution how, try as they might, they haven't been able to cut your trail out yonder, you poor lone wolf!"

The Fargo Kid was too busy coming again to answer, just then. But as they shared a bottle and a Havana claro, afterwards, he naturally grumbled, "So it's *Roy* already? Fess up, you put out to him, upstairs, just now, didn't you?"

She protested, "I commenced to cry when he tried to feel my titty, you jealous thing. I told you how easy it would be to string along a married man without having to go all the way with him. Tell me why you call Crimp Gooding *Crimp*. Does he walk with a limp, in case I see him first at some distance?"

The Fargo Kid grumbled, "He ain't crippled up and he walks taller than me as well, dad blast that false-hearted Trixie! I mean, I've watched old Crimp take a leak and he ain't got nothing to offer a gal that *I* don't have. Why did she let him talk her into testicating in court against me like that?"

"Maybe he has a longer tongue, or simply a slicker way of talking with it. As I followed your case in the papers, Crimp made a deal to collect and spend the bounty on you with all charges against himself and those others dropped by the state. I'm still waiting to hear why you nicknamed him Crimp."

The Fargo Kid passed the bottle to her as he said, "I never. He had the handle when we met up, long after the war. He got the title back east, crimping or gathering recruits for both sides. He'd jumped the hundred dollar enlistment bounty himself, more than once. But to make it pay off, serious, old Crimp sent squads of eager country boys to fight for the north or south. He'd often send the same bunch to both sides until he saw a hundred dollars in Union greenbacks was going to be worth more, once the Union won."

He took an expansive drag on their cigar and added, "In any case, once he'd set things up, Crimp split the enlistment bounty with his innocent-looking knockaround hairpins and hid them out when they all deserted, along with guns, boots and such Crimp could sell, a month after they'd enlisted and drawn their first handsome hundred and thirteen dollars off the paybook."

He thoughtfully added, "When you study on it, Crimp Gooding has ever been a lying two-faced son of a bitch, and I should have had my head examined for taking him under my wing and introducing him to my warm natured ladylove!"

The much bigger woman he'd been warming up since getting out of jail confided, "Some girls are swayed by slick-talking jaspers. Some are just fickle. Some are just sluts, like me. Before you scold me, little darling, consider the edge that's going to give me when, not if, I catch up with the slick-talking Crimp Gooding. He's not going to be on the prod for anyone like me. Your Trixie has established him as a skirt chasing rogue who'd fuck a pal's woman. I know where he's headed. There's only one place up the Arkansas a money-hungry cuss with an eye for the ladies could be headed. I won't have to hunt high and low for him in Leadville. I stand out in a crowd, and at the risk of sounding immodest, a stranger in an expensive town will be inclined to gravitate to a target such as I."

The Fargo Kid rested his free hand in the dark blond thatch between her massive thighs as he chortled, "You sound like you already know old Crimp, Creasy. I can see how he might hope to lose himself on the busy streets of that brawling mining camp, and I can see how he might notice someone like you in any crowd. But then what? Even if you can get him alone, Crimp Gooding's big, dangerous and suspicious natured. You ain't going to be able to shoot him in his sleep because old Crimp never sleeps with anybody else in the same room with him."

Increase Younger yawned languidly and suggested, "How would you like to eat my pussy some more, kid?"

When he protested he didn't have his second wind yet, she said she just wanted to teach him a new trick. So the Fargo Kid set aside the bottle and cigar to roll over on his hands and knees, facedown betwixt her titanic legs as she spread her huge thighs in wide welcome.

The Fargo Kid was encouraged by the faint scent of vinegar as he lowered his face to her groin and gingerly commenced to tongue her pink clit. Then she'd suddenly crossed her knees to trap his head between her big muscular thighs and bury his face deep in her wet crotch as she laughingly teased, "How do you like it so far, lover? Can you breathe enough to stay alive while I crack your skull like a walnut?"

The Fargo Kid, strong and wiry for his size, couldn't breathe in or out as he flailed at the outside of her massive legs at an awkward angle whilst little white stars swarmed like gnats behind his closed eyelids and the pressure on his trapped skull increased painfully.

Then she relaxed her death-grip to croon, "Can't get much licking from a dead man. So do me right, and I'll let you live."

As the Fargo Kid commenced to French her with ardor

born in part from desperation, she mused, thighs far apart, "My, that does feel nice, and what if I got Crimp Gooding to go down on me and make me come just before I crushed his skull all the way. How do you like the notion of his dying with me satisfied and him still wishing in vain?"

The Fargo Kid liked the notion so well he sincerely licked her all the way to climax before he mounted her again to satisfy himself.

But a hundred miles off, in Denver, Longarm and Portia Parkhurst, Esquire were barely getting started, even though they both knew how things had to turn out betwixt pals who'd already fornicated more 'n once. For despite her being a lawyer, the lean and hungry-looking attorney at law had been raised by Victorian standards of ladylike behavior. So Longarm had to treat her to six acts of vaudeville at the Apollo after spaghetti and meatballs at Romanos before she felt obliged to invite him in for a nightcap once he'd walked her home.

As they went through the charade of highballs for two in Portia's front parlor, they ran out of things to say about the Jensen claim, and he wound up explaining what he'd been doing out yonder to begin with.

Portia agreed Billy Vail had been wise to surround Longarm with a more open field of fire until they determined whether "that unfortunate woman fresh from her dreary prison cell" had been serious about killing him or not. Portia liked to feel there was some good in everybody and suggested a few weeks of freedom and perhaps a new boyfriend might have made the poor bitter thing more mellow than when she'd sat down to declare war on him in writing.

Demurely sipping bourbon and fizz water, the no-longer-young and hence right-worldly lawyer observed, "I tell all my clients to always set a letter aside and read it the next day, after a good night's sleep and a warm meal, before they post it. Things we put down on paper in the heat of anger can read awfully foolish, even when we mean them."

Longarm said, "I pointed that out to Billy Vail. He pointed out to me that insanity tended to run in families and reminded me of the troubles we had with Increase Younger's murderous clan, so far. That baby brother she's still complaining about was sneaky and treacherous beyond the call of duty. Long before we met up on the South Pass range, he'd somehow managed to convince everyone for miles around he was a South Pass country rider who'd been working for years as an honest top-hand-cum-foreman for a cattle baroness who had more important worries on her mind."

"Was she pretty?" Portia quietly but firmly demanded.

He shrugged and said, "She made a habit of marrying up with spouse abusers. Assuming the local nickname of Timberline, Cotton Younger had taken up her cause, and we all thought he was right gallant until he turned out to be a two-faced killer. The point I'm making about a branch of the Younger family neither Bob, Cole nor Jim Younger want a thing to do with is that they run to deadly as diamondbacks but more patient than you'd expect a Paiute laying for a rabbit or a spider in its woodshed web to behave. Billy Vail says, and I had to agree, we'd best find out where in thunder the big gal is, and what she might be up to, before we write her death threat off as scribbled in haste."

"Don't you have any idea where she might be, right now?" Portia asked as she moved to freshen his tall drink.

Longarm placed his free hand over the highball glass to prevent her as he replied, "We know she was up to Jimtown near Trapper's Rock a spell back. We know somebody big and blond enough to pass for her checked in and out of the Dexter Hotel more recent, without leav-

ing a forwarding address. If she's still in town, she's staying in some private home with kith or kin. If she ain't in
town no more, we don't have anything to worry about.
She's not wanted on any charges, state or federal, save
for threatening to murder a public official, namely me. If
she sniffed around at the notion and decided to move on
after she'd had time to reconsider, I'd be as willing to
forgive and forget.

"Are you trying to get me drunk, Miss Portia?" Longarm asked.

The lean figure in courthouse-black poplin reached up
to unpin her silver-streaked black hair with a Mona Lisa
smile as she soberly told him, "You're right. Hard liquor
may loosen up a properly raised young lady, but as many
a bride who's filed for annulment has assured me, a man
who's swigged enough to sing 'Aura Lee' in public can
be nothing but a bother to a girl in bed!"

Longarm set his glass aside, swung around to get a
sudden grasp on the situation and rose with Portia craddled in his arms before she got finished asking, "Just what
do you think you're doing, Deputy Long?"

He just craddled her closer and headed for the bedroom,
knowing his way from earlier visits. So Portia removed
his Stetson to skim it across the room and laugh like a
kid before she remembered herself and told him he was
just awful.

He didn't ask, this time, whether or not she wanted him
to put her down and just be on his way. He didn't like to
see a woman cry the way they cried when they felt all
mixed up and torn betwixt what their mommas had told
them and what their bodies were telling them. He just
spread her atop the covers across her four poster, shucked
his coat and six-gun, and proceeded to haul her crinkly
black skirts high, knowing from experience he'd find her
wearing nothing above the black lace garters holding up
her black silk stockings.

Portia knew he knew what he'd find betwixt her legs because she'd planned things that way, and she knew he knew she'd planned things that way. So she suddenly found herself blurting, "Wouldn't it be much more sensible if we just got undressed, first, and just . . . you know, got down to it the way we did that last time, dear?"

So for once she saved them both a heap of bother, albeit later that night they both wound up with rug burns, once he had her really warmed up.

Chapter 8

Portia Parkhurst, Esquire was an early riser. So was Longarm that particular Tuesday morn, once he opened his eyes to find the long lean lawyer astride his naked hips with the dawn light soft on her bounding bare breasts. It was a caution how passionate skinny gals with ample tits seemed by nature. She naturally tried to blame it all on him as soon as they'd come the more passionate way, with him on top.

But she was a good sport about being used, abused and ravaged, as she put it, and served him scrambled eggs with buttered toast and high-toned imported marmalade in bed, with enough black coffee to get them both going.

So once they'd torn off another piece as they showered together, they got dressed to get going. She let him tag along to the land office. It meant he'd get to his own office late, of course, but in spite of his threats to the contrary, Billy Vail had never really fired him for blowing in just in time to go to lunch.

Longarm had signed a process-serving form and hung on to the Land Office summons after little Pia had translated it for her mother out to the Jensen homestead. So Portia handed it back it their reception clerk with a form of her own, allowing she was there to answer for a client who didn't speak English and hadn't done anything.

As Longarm had suspected, the land office only wanted to know how come nobody had been answering any forms they'd sent out to the Widow Jensen. They also wanted a death certificate for their files.

Before Longarm could put a foot in his mouth, Portia produced a properly filled out, if informally witnessed and signed, standard death certificate and a power of attorney the Widow Jensen would find out she'd signed when and if she got around to asking. Longarm knew you seldom got in trouble with friendly forgery nobody challenged.

The land office clerk they were jawing with seemed satisified and when he produced a form of their own for the widow to fill out and sign in front of a notary public, Portia filled it out atop their counter, signed in the widow's name and produced her own notary seal to notarize the same. When the older man asked if she was allowed to do that, Longarm confided, "It's best not to challenge this lawyer, pard. I've watched her in court. It's painful to see grown men blush rose red and stammer like schoolboys without newspaper men taking down every word of their mortification to amuse their readers."

The land office cuss shrugged and said it was no skin off his nose unless somebody challenged the Jensen claim in court on his or her own. So once they had all the papers to mail to the widow, addressed to her English-speaking daughter, Longarm said she was counting on Longarm to lick the stamps and allowed she had to get on over to the state supreme court where a working girl could make some *money*.

They shook and kissed on that out in the hallway, and parted right friendly around nine-thirty. So once he'd dropped by the Parthenon for a beer and some pickled pig's feet to top off Portia's sort of delicate breakfast, it was only a little after ten when Longarm got to his own office. So old Henry, the pallid young squirt who played the typewriter out front, had no call to shoot Longarm one of those Now-you're-going-to-get-it! looks.

Longarm smiled thinly and observed in passing, "It ain't true we're paid by the hour, Henry, and even if we were, I got an excuse this morning."

Henry muttered, "*That*'s something new around here!" as Longarm got on back to Billy Vail's inner sanctum.

As he entered, his superior shot a glance at the banjo clock on one wall to exclaim, "So good of you to grace us with your presence, old son. The only thing saving your ass this time is the mellow mood I'm in this morning."

He leaned back in his swivel chair to add, "Sometime I get so smart I'm tempted to propose to myself! I was just fixing to toss an all-points in the wastebasket when a more brilliant thought occured to me!"

Billy Vail had yet to invite Longarm to sit down and light up. But since there was a horsehair and leather visitor's chair and no ashtray evident on his side of the desk, the younger lawman sat down, uninvited, and lit a cheroot to defend himself against Billy Vail's cigar before he asked what made the old fart feel so all-fired smart.

Vail said, "Road agent and bank robber named Tone Cunningham aka the Fargo Kid just busted out of the Pueblo County Jail with the help of some friends. Late at night with long knives, Apache style. Pueblo County seems mighty upset about this. Can't say I blame 'em, but as of first glance the Fargo Kid ain't wanted federal. So what say we take a *second* glance?"

Longarm flicked tobacco ash on the rug, ignoring the dirty look from his boss, as he replied, "I give up. What did this knife-fighting rascal do that was federal?"

Vail said, "Nothing. Him and his gang specialized in stagecoach robberies or modest sums from small-town banks. They never hit any post office, government payroll or even a soldier blue. Somebody must have wised Cunningham up the one time he went to prison for all too short a spell, and, damn it, Custis, that's my *rug* you're scattering all them ashes on!"

Longarm said, "Heard-tell tobacco ash kills carpet mites, and I got to flick ash *some* damned place! How were we fixing to charge this murderous small-time crook as a federal want, boss?"

Vail said, "We ain't. I'm sending you out of town to pick up another no-good bastard the Fargo Kid has declared he intends to kill. Since justice is blind, when it suits the prosecution, another crook riding with the Fargo Kid a spell was granted immunity in exchange for his testimony in the Kid's murder trial. His gang of three and a doxy they may have been sharing never amassed a great fortune. But they killed a bank messenger and a prosperous gambler they were robbing in the state of Colorado. Both victims were heavily insured. So the bounties added up, and the Kid's hasty trigger finger might have been getting on the nerves of his associates. At any rate, they turned him in for the prices on his head and immunity from prosecution. One can understand how this must have pissed the Fargo Kid considerable."

Longarm said, "I know it would piss *me*. But what's the federal charge?"

Billy Vail said, "By the time you catch up with him, I feel sure we'll have a fresh warrant on one of the former pals the Fargo Kid is stalking with murder in the first in mind. They call one Alvin Gooding—*Crimp* Gooding—because, during the war, he played both sides false by crimping bounty jumpers in wholesale numbers. How do you like it so far?"

Longarm made a wry face and replied, "It ain't going to work. Where would we ever find a federal judge who wouldn't throw such a case out of court at this late date? For Pete's sake, Billy, President Hayes has granted full amnesty to irregulars who rode with Quantrill, long as they promised not to do that no more! The statute of limitations has run out on wartime deserters, so . . ."

"So don't interrupt when your elders are speaking," Billy Vail cut in, taking advantage of Longarm's bemused silence to explain, "I've yet to order you to arrest Crimp Gooding as a professional deserter. I'm ordering you to bring him in as a material witness, federal, because he knows where a whole lot of War Department bounty money wound up, see?"

Longarm laughed and said, "If you can sell *that* to the accounting office, I got this gold mine in the Big Rock Candy Mountains I've been trying to unload. If you need an excuse to send me down Pueblo way, why don't you just order me to help Pueblo County catch that escaped prisoner, the Fargo Kid?"

Vail shook his head and replied, "That might be tougher to sell. I used to try common sense on the powers that be, but I've found it way easier to confound them with legalese, and so, as I was saying, I want you to run down to Pueblo and see if you can round up Crimp Gooding as a possible material witness, federal, before that Fargo Kid can kill him under Colorado jurisdiction. Don't matter whether Gooding knows where all that money went or not. It's going to take you some time to round him up whether anybody wants to question him about the money, the snows of yesteryear or the morals of the late Lola Montez out Frisco way."

Longarm said, "I'll go. But how long do you expect me to shilly-shally around Pueblo, for Pete's sake? Where do I pick Crimp Gooding up?"

Vail slyly replied, "Hard to say. The sheriff down yonder says they ain't seen hide nor hair of the poor simp since he got his own death threats from a pal he betrayed. He may be even more worried about the unknown quantity that busted the Fargo Kid out of jail down yonder.

Sheriff says nobody knew the Fargo Kid had *other* pals that dangerous. Crimp Gooding, another sidekick called Mel Stuart and a wild redhead they call Trixie Davis thought they were the whole gang when they ratted on the Fargo Kid. One can see why they might be running scared, now. Sheriff says Mel Stuart and the redhead are still holed up on a spread just outside Pueblo. Crimp Gooding and the runt sworn to kill him could be most anywheres right now."

Longarm demanded, "Billy, are you sending me on a snipe hunt just to get me out of town?"

To which Vail could only reply with a boyish grin and a wave of his smoldering stogie, "Yeah, ain't I a sly old dog? I don't see how in thunder you'll find Crimp Gooding all that soon, either. But I feel certain you'll give it the old college try. You might want to interview those other potential federal witnesses, Stuart and the gal. In the meantime, we'll keep watching out for that amazon after your ass up *this* way, secure in the certainty we don't have to worry about her spotting you in Denver before we spot *her* in Denver, see?"

Longarm did and had to allow Vail's plan had shooting it out sudden with a woman beat.

Neither Longarm nor Billy Vail had any way of knowing what the six-foot-six woman in question was saying at that very moment to the Fargo Kid, down in that secret cellar room.

"There's a northbound combination leaving for Denver and points north around seven, when the gloaming will have everything and everybody purple, gold and fuzzy. Roy Manx has assured me they're watching trains coming *in* to Pueblo. They're not expecting the notorious Fargo Kid to be *leaving* Pueblo before he makes a play for his former flame and Mel Stuart, being used as bait by the lawmen staked out all around that livery spread a serious walk from the railroad depot.

"I want you out back in the carriage house at sundown. Roy Manx will be dropping by about then on his way home. It'll only take me a jiffy to find out whether they've made any changes in plans. If you don't see me waving a fan at myself in the kitchen window, you'll know it's safe for you to make a run for it, at a sedate stroll. You won't want to board that northbound until you hear the engine's bell tolling all aboard. You'll want to give them time to fish-eye everyone getting *off* that train, earlier, so's they won't be interested in anybody getting on.

"I have some written instructions for you, here. I stopped off in Denver on my way south just long enough to determine, without going near the son of a bitch, that Longarm rooms alone in a shabby neighborhood southwest of Cherry Creek and drops by the Parthenon Saloon near the federal building for their free lunch, around noon. After hours he's just as likely to frequent the less expensive Black Cat, closer to the stock yards. I tried to get a line on his ladyloves. It would be nice if you could shoot him in bed with a woman and disgrace him in the *Denver Post* and *Rocky Mountain News*. But though they say he's a heller with the ladies, he's one of those discreet bastards who declines to brag to the other kids about their slap and tickle."

She sighed wistfully and added, "Just my luck that the only man I know who doesn't kiss and tell is a man I've sworn to kill or have killed. Don't you go bragging on *my* ass before this is all over and done with if you ever expect to meet up with me in Cheyenne as we've planned!"

The Fargo Kid said, "I ain't no kiss-and-tell! Have you ever heard me say Trixie Davis likes to take it in the ass?"

She laughed and pointed out, "You just did. I *thought* you'd picked up such inclinations in prison. I'd better get up and get dressed for the company I'm expecting this evening, lover."

The Fargo Kid pouted, "I'll bet that married deputy brags about all the stuff he has lined up on the side. No offense, but there's a lot of you to line up, and, no shit, are you really going to let that Roy Manx have his wicked way with you, Creasy?"

She rose, a lot, to slip into her Turkish toweling robe as she told the man who'd just had his own wicked way with her, "I told you. I *have* to. Once you're *gone*, I mean. It's not that I like him *better* than you, honey bunny; I need his betrayal as my alibi. I want Longarm to know, or to think he knows, I'm the one who killed him as he gasps for breath once you've gut-shot him as per instructions. But since I'd as soon not pay for the crime, I mean to make sure I can prove I was a hundred miles or more from the scene of the crime at the time of his protracted death!"

The Fargo Kid marveled, "You're sure mean-hearted for such a purdy little thing. But before you bestow any of that swell pussy on that literally fucking lawman, have you considered what a fix you'll be in if he kisses and never tells?"

The imperious natural blond with auburn hair sniffed knowingly, "Married men *always* brag when they cheat on their wives. What point would there be in cheating on that wife if he didn't get to say he was a hell of rogue?"

She frowned thoughtfully as she softly added, half to herself, "A single man who respects the women he makes love to may be able to keep his mouth shut. *He's* fornicating just because it feels good, not to put one over on a poor foolish woman who trusts him. But, *trust me*, Roy Manx won't be able to keep it to himself once I give him a French lesson he's never had from any girl who saved her all for the church wedding she was able to hold out for!"

Then she caught herself and snapped, "What am I mooning about, for Gawd's sake? I don't care why Longarm doesn't kiss and tell! I want you to get your ass up yonder and shoot him in the guts for me and my poor baby brother, the only man I ever . . . felt sisterly about."

The Fargo Kid softly murmured, "Holy . . . shit! So *that*'s how come you hate that one lawman so much!"

Increase Younger snapped, "Don't ask nosey quesions! Just gut-shoot the big bastard, and we'll talk about how come when we meet up again in Cheyenne, hear?"

Chapter 9

Visitors to the smokey industrial complex of Pueblo, Colorado, were forever asking where the pueblo might be. But there had never been a pueblo in Pueblo in the sense Anglos used the term for a multistory freestone or adobe structure erected by so-called Pueblo Indians.

The early Spanish speakers of New Mexico had dubbed all sorts of Hopi, Tanoan, Zuni and such they caught living in brick- or stone-walled settlements "Pueblo Indians." But the Comanche summer camp near the junction of Fountain Creek and the Arkansas River, within easy riding of the Front Range, had most likely resembled a mighty big tipi ring when, along about the time John Paul Jones was declaring he had just begun to fight, the Spanish governor of New Mexico, Don Juan Bautista de Anza, declared he'd had just about enough of the horse-thieving, hell-raising *chingado* Comanche under their whooping and hollering Chief Green Horn, described in Spanish as *Cuerno Verde*, of course.

As in the case of the so-called Sioux, *Comanche* was a nickname they'd been given by their enemies, in this case Uto-Aztec speakers whose phrase, *Ko-man-Chica* translates best as "constant enemy."

So Governor de Anza rode east through Raton Pass that summer with as many Indian as Spanish riders in his 600-man column.

Along the way they whupped and captured a Comanche-hunting band and learned from their prisoners how Green Horn and the main body of his nation had returned from a raid rich with frisky ponies and weeping women, to celebrate with a swell party where the town of Pueblo would later rise. But they had to get there, first, and so de Anza got there firster, mopped up the few hostiles in sight and dug in to ambush the returning raiders.

The results were an earlier version of Little Big Horn with the white boys and their Indian allies *winning* that one. New Mexican history would record the results as the Battle of Cuerno Verde, albeit hardly anybody on the winning side got hurt. Green Horn, his son, four other Comanche chiefs and their boss, Medicine Man, were cut down like summer hay in a fusillade of fire from hidden positions. The de Anza solution to "the Indian problem" resulted in a generation of peace before the Comanche recovered their sass.

The site of the Comanche summer camp was indicated on Spanish survey maps as, what else, a *pueblo*. So the name stuck as the handy site grew from a trading post to what the local chamber of commerce liked to describe as "the Pittsburgh of the West," and if that was laying it on a tad, it wasn't for lack of trying. The way-smaller but still growing communitity of Pueblo inhaled goods and services from all over to exhale coal and smelted metals from gold through pig iron to lead and zinc, along with hides, wool and meat on the hoof from the sea of grass every direction but West.

So to say Pueblo, Colorado, was a gritty confusion under a constant haze of coal smoke within easy distance of its rail yards was not an overstatement. Hence, had Longarm and the Fargo Kid been passing on opposite sides of

Union Avenue, they'd have been likely to be unaware of one another as metal shops clamored, hammer mills hammered and smelter stacks roared like man-made volcanos all around.

But in point of fact, the Fargo Kid was still hiding out in that hired carriage house as Longarm got down from the afternoon southbound, this time loaded for bear with his heavily laden McClellan saddle braced on his hip just behind his six-gun by his left hand.

As he strode northeast toward the junction where Union, Main and First Street blurred into one another in a haze of dust and cussing teamsters, his saddlebags, bedroll and Winchester '73 naturally came along with his saddle. So, first things coming first, he checked into a hotel he knew of old near Fourth and Main to unload before he had a sit-down beer, Walter's brand being more available than Coors in Colorado's second city. Then, he went on over to the courthouse square on Santa Fe Avenue, just west of north-south Fountain Creek.

He had no way of knowing, as he moseyed into the sheriff's office for a courtesy call, their Deputy Manx had just left for the day, a tad early, to tear off some quiff on the side before he got home a tad late for supper.

Rank having its privileges, the sheriff had left even earlier than a senior deputy who'd been waiting for him to leave, for Pete's sake. So Longarm was stuck with the night shift, and vice versa, but they were able to bring him up to date on their manhunt and give him the written directions he needed to that livery and stud spread off to the east of town. They said nobody had seen hide nor hair of Crimp Gooding since he'd come in all upset about that death threat from the recently escaped Fargo Kid. Longarm felt no call to ask them about a six-foot-six woman penning death threats. So he didn't. Lawmen got used to such mail, penned all too often by all sorts of cranks and on occasion by somebody who really meant it.

He just thanked them, and then, seeing it seemed an awkward hour to call on folk you weren't fixing to arrest, and since *he* ate supper, too, Longarm ambled back to his hotel, where he knew they had a fair dining room serving tolerable grub on the American plan.

That was where you got your room and three meals a day at a set rate. It could save you money if the hotel kitchen knew what it was doing, albeit, most places, Longarm followed the European plan, or "alley cart," as they said it fancy in French, so's he could pick and choose what he ate, most often off the premises. But the good old Lake George Hotel, albeit four or five miles from the lake it was named for, served a tolerable soup-to-nuts sit-down on its American plan. So he went on upstairs to tote soap and a fresh shirt to wash up and see if he could come out looking more like a white man after that sooty train ride down from Denver. They left the windows open in warm weather, bless their grimy souls.

Stripping to the waist before a basin, Longarm soon had his hands and face clean enough for polite society. He'd shaved that afternoon before leaving Denver. He washed under his arms as well, and dried with the stale shirt before he donned the fresh one, smelling faintly of the cedar shavings he kept in his saddlebags to discourage bugs.

Thanks to the current federal dress code of the Hayes Reform Administration, Longarm was required to sport a sissy shoestring tie with his three-piece suit. But he meant to have supper on his own time and the infernal tie could wait 'til he got to feeling *official* some more. He suspected they might frown on his entering their dining room hatless in just his vest and shirtsleeves, but the smokey afternoon atmosphere felt mighty stuffy in warm weather, and if they didn't want his custom, he'd just check out and find more comfortable quarters for this pointless visit.

Buttoning his shirt most of the way up, Longarm left

the washroom with the damp discarded shirt in his left hand. So his right hand was free, as it was supposed to be, when Longarm spotted an awesome sight moving down the hallway ahead with her back to him.

It made no sense, and her pinned-up hair looked black. But Billy Vail had warned she could be circling, that she was known to use hair coloring, and how many women that size could there *be* on your average continent?

So Longarm drew and threw down on the titanic hour-glass figure in summer-weight maroon taffeta with the bodice buttoned down the back as far as the Dolly Varden skirts. He was light on his feet, and she must not have known he was there, going by the startled gasp she let out when he gently but firmly placed the muzzle of his .44-40 against her spine to order her in a tone of command to see if she could touch the ceiling for him.

As she showed him she could, she protested in a sultry contralto tone, "I don't have any money on me. My purse is in Room two-B."

Longarm smiled thinly and replied, "Two-B or not two-B is not the question, ma'am. This ain't a stickup. I'm the law."

She started to turn, then decided not to when he poked her spine harder with his six-gun, and gasped, "I haven't done anything against the law, good sir! You must have me mixed up with someone else!"

Longarm said, "That's possible, ma'am. Now, I'd like you to place them palms against yonder wall, move your feet back my way a pace and spread your legs so's I can pat you down for a Gatling gun or worse!"

She moved to obey his voice of command, but even as she assumed the position she complained, "This is ridiculous as well as awfully undignified! What if someone else should come along to find us here like this and . . . *¡Aye que indecente!* How many women conceal a weapon *there?*"

83

He assured her she'd be surprised as he made sure she didn't have a thigh-holster further down, politely asking, "*¿Habla 'Spanol, senorita?*"

She said, "Of course. I am the Widow Garson, Consuela Garson from Santa Fe, but my maiden name was Vallejo! Who on earth do you *think* I might be, good sir?"

Longarm said, "I'm still working on that. You can put your hands down, seeing you can't be packing any concealed weapons. Then why don't we mosey on down to *my* room, two-C, to see what *else* we might be able to work out, seeing my room's closer, and I won't have to worry about you reaching in a drawer."

As she preceded him gracefully down the hall, considering her imposing height, he explained, "You answer the description of a recent graduate of an Iowa institution for wayward women, no offense. It's true they describe her as a natural blond of likely Scotch-Irish descent. But any drug store sells brunette hair dye, and if *I* know some Border Mex, most anybody could fake as much or more. Step down the hall a pace whilst I unlock my own door, ma'am. Are you in the habit of leaving your purse untended in your own hired room?"

She said, "I was only going down the hall to . . . use the facilities. I never considered the danger of prowlers in a respectable hotel. I suppose you must think I'm pretty country."

He repeated he was still working on what he considered her as he opened his door and waved her in. As she preceded him, he tossed his damp shirt across the saddle draped over the foot of the brass bedstead and lowered his gun muzzle to a friendlier position as the gal of say thirty either way turned to face him as she demanded, "Do I look Scotch-Irish, for heaven's sake?"

Longarm kicked the door shut behind him as he soberly replied to her sensible question. "You don't look all that Mexican, either. At the risk of turning your head, Miss

Consuela, you've no doubt been informed that your regular features don't add up to any of the inbred peasant populations vaudeville comics identify as Irish, Scotch, Dutch or whatever. This anthropology gal I used to know says inbred village folk tend to look particular, whilst the folk we call aristocratic look much the same, and sort of handsome, no matter where they hail from."

She tried not to sound smug as she confessed, "Well, I *am* a Lopez y Cortez on my mother's side."

Longarm said, "Somebody on one side or the other must have been a mite taller than average. Aristocrats or folk descended from peasants from different old counties tend to have them same regular features as older family traits cancel one another out. So to tell the truth, I only have your word that you'd be the Widow Garson of Santa Fe and not the six-foot-six Increase Younger from other parts entire!"

The tall shapely brunette pouted, "I'm only six foot four, and I've never heard of your Increases whatever, good sir. I can't say I haven't wished I'd stopped growing a little sooner, but this is the first time I've ever been accused of being *unlawfully* tall!"

Longarm laughed and assured her, "Your height ain't a federal offense, ma'am. The lady I sincerely hope you ain't stands guilty of a signed death threat addressed to yours truly, Deputy U.S. Marshal Custis Long."

She didn't do a thing to dispel his natural suspicion as she blinked in surprise, smiled radiantly, and said, "I know who you are! The simple people of *La Raza* call you *el Brazo Largo* down on the border! You should be ashamed of yourself if half the things they say about you are true. But no man whose wanted dead or alive by *El Presidente Diaz* can be all bad, and you can ask any Mexican this close to Santa Fe about *me*!"

Longarm smiled thinly and decided, "That could take time and be a bother. Just hold your horses and give us time to work something out. I've yet to have my supper, either, and I'll be proud to help you to a seat down to the dining room as soon as we convince me you ain't the one and original Increase Younger!"

She asked exactly what the other woman looked like.

He wearily replied, "That's the problem. My boss, Marshal Vail, has sent to Iowa State for her rogue's gallery photographs. But that'll take days. I wish there was some way to send photographs by telegraph wire, but there ain't. So all we know for certain is that my life has been threatened by a big old good-looking gal, and I fear that fits you tighter than any other gal I've laid eyes on lately!"

She asked him to repeat that part about Increase Younger being a natural blond.

He nodded but said, "She's known to dye her hair all sorts of other shades."

Consuela Garson, demurely but confidently proclaimed, "I'm not a natural blond. I'm a natural brunette. Allow me to show you, good sir!"

Then she did, reaching down to haul her skirts high enough to expose her creamy bare flesh from the garters of her silk stockings to her deeply indented belly button, and she sure was right fuzzy for a gal!

As she dropped her skirts to once more hide her jet black pubic apron, she was blushing, but managed to sound calm as she asked Longarm if he was satisfied.

To which Longarm could only reply, "Not hardly, but you've surely convinced me you ain't no natural *blond*. So allow me to apologize, and I'd be proud to explain further if you'd care to join me for a late supper, downstairs."

Chapter 10

Since Longarm had stayed there before, Consuela suggested he order for both of them from the limited menu. He didn't ask if she let the man take the lead when she danced. He suspected most of the time it would be up to her. He warned himself it was early to worry whether he could lick her fair and square in an honestly contested wrassle.

He told her their onion soup and blue plate combination of roast beef, mashed spuds with gravy and buttered sparrow grass had been tolerable, last time. She said that sounded jake with her, and so he asked if she took her coffee with her grub or after. When she said she followed the Spanish custom of coffee with dessert, he ordered the same, along with extra ice water to get himself through like a sport.

He could see she was as country as himself when she dug into her blue plate without the table patter of some society gals he'd eaten with in the past. But as they relaxed more over coffee and raisin cake dessert, she wanted to hear more about that natural blond she'd proven she couldn't be.

Longarm tersely explained how he'd had to shoot it out with the big gal's brother out Salt Lake way, leaving out some gory details in consideration of another lady's feelings at the table.

Consuela decided, "She wasn't fair in blaming *you*, Custis. When a man chooses of his own free will to ride the Primrose Path, he has nobody but himself to blame when, not if, the law catches up with him. You say they gave the creature ten years in prison to ponder the error of her ways, and she *still* wants to be an outlaw, now that she doesn't have to? She must be *loco en la cabeza*!"

"My words exactly, earlier," Longarm replied. He washed down some raisin cake and added, "Some folk collect stamps, some folk build ships in bottles and other folk lead disgusting lives. Read this yarn a spell back about a Miss Carmilla, an immortal vampire with all sorts of magic powers. It was just a made-up story, of course, and there's no such a thing as a vampire. But reading about Miss Carmilla, I was surely reminded of many a poor soul who just can't help acting needlessly disgusting!"

She dimpled across the table to observe, "I might have known you'd bring up yet another woman, *el Brazo Largo*. What did this vampire do to disgust you so?"

He said, "I'd rather not say whilst we're eating. My point is that like Miss Increase Younger, she didn't *have* to. It says right in the story how she had everlasting youth, untold wealth and all sorts of magical powers. So, had she wanted to, she could have lived high on the hog in a fashionable neighborhood and gone to all the fancy balls in town dressed in the latest fashions. Being one of them vampire gals, she couldn't be about in broad daylight and had to sleep all day 'til the sun went down again. But she didn't have to sleep . . . where she slept in that disturbing story. So she must have *wanted* to carry on disgusting, like a lot of outlaws who seem just as twisted up inside.

Miss Carmilla didn't have to act so unnatural in other ways, either. I mean, sure, she was on a peculiar diet, being a vampire and all, but she could have satisfied it without hurting other *folk*. And her . . . ah, love life struck me as a perfect waste of her beautiful immortal flesh!"

"What did she *do*?" asked the young and beautiful widow woman.

Longarm shook his head and insisted, "Not at the table. Maybe some time when I know you better, and you ain't just et!"

So they finished their suppers and went for an evening stroll along nearby Fountain Creek under the sullen red sky-glow of the smelters all around. Where it wasn't lined with black satanic mills, Fountain Creek ran through stretches of box elder, choke cherry, cottonwood, willow and such, with cinder paths laid out, and hither and yon a park bench to sit and admire the night sounds from nearby crickets to distant stamping mills.

Consuela allowed she needed a rest before they'd walked all that far. So they sat in the inky shade of an overhead willow, and he had to listen to the familiar story of her short happy married life and all the trials and tribulations of a widow stuck with running her late husband's prosperous freight operation. She was in Pueblo that night with a view to a new wagon route betwixt Pueblo and Santa Fe. When Longarm didn't argue about that, she brought up that story about Miss Carmilla, the disgusting vampire gal. Consuela seemed bound and determined to hear why *el Brazo Largo* of all people had found her so sassy.

Longarm said, "Well, to begin with, having all the time and money it might have taken her to find a better place to bed down when the sun was shining, she chose to sleep in a coffin, a coffin filled to the brim with *blood*."

"You mean she slept *in* the blood, like a pickled pig's foot soaking in brine?"

He nodded and explained, "The vampire expert who was after her said she had to be soaked in blood, inside and out, to stay immortal. But she'd have avoided a heap of trouble had she bought a slaughter house with her unlimited wealth and left *human* blood where it was."

Consuela decided, "Maybe she had to be soaked in human blood. You say she drank it, too? What if she couldn't help it? What if the spell only worked with human blood?"

He shrugged and said, "She had other disturbing habits that caused trouble for her. Trouble for the author, too. His book was declared obscene, and you couldn't buy it openly in Boston town or heaps of other places because he'd made Miss Carmilla so . . . disturbing."

"You mean she had worse habits than sucking and bathing in human blood?" the big brunette marveled, leaning closer as if they were to share some dirty secrets.

Longarm said, "Yep, and like I said, her chosen way of life makes no sense unless you allow some folk are just born ornery and grow up contrary for the sake of *being* contrary."

But when Consuela pressed him for the dirty details, Longarm told her, "Let's just say she enjoyed upsetting others. We don't know one another well enough to talk openly about, ah, crimes against nature."

The big strong brunette took him by the left wrist and guided his hand to her heroic right breast, husking, "Do you feel you know me better, now?"

He put his other arm around her and reeled her in for a kiss, as most men would have. She kissed back as if she hadn't been getting any lately, with considerable skill, and guided his hand down the front of her tight bodice to explore the loose folds of her lap, spreading her big thighs just enough to allow his hand was welcome down yonder. He already knew she wore nothing under the summerweight Dolly Varden. So he got a good grip on her situation, through the taffeta, before he confided, with his lips still touching hers, "Miss Carmilla didn't just suck blood out of other gals. She licked 'em all over and made them climax against their religions and wills so's she could set 'em up for a hard time in the hereafter before she finished killing 'em. Like I said, evil for the sake of evil. She wasn't interested in men or lizzy gals who *wanted* her to love 'em up. So she had it coming when they found her secret tomb in broad day and fixed her good. Anyone with a lick of sense could see she'd have been better off using all her powers *sensible*. But natural-born moral monsters are like that. Have you ever asked yourself why a witch woman with magic powers would *choose* to live deep in a swamp in some shanty filled with spider webs and let herself look like a scary old crone when *mortal* women with a little pin money of their own and a little powder and perfume can make themselves look right presentable?"

She snuggled closer and began to gather her skirts up out of his way as she purred, "You've convinced me. Your Increase Younger must be a very sorry mess, and what are you *doing* to me, *el Brazo Largo?*"

"Didn't you know?" might have sounded sardonic. So he kissed her some more, got two fingers in her, and pulled back, "I could do you better back at the hotel with these stuffy clothes out of our way."

She said, "Oh, no, I couldn't go back to your room with you, knowing right out that you mean to have your wicked way with me!"

As he finger fucked her, he dryly asked where she'd gotten such an outlandish notion. She spread her thighs wider to let him probe deeper, and then she suddenly crossed her thighs, nearly spraining his wrist, as she sobbed he had to be strong for the both of them.

Longarm removed his hand—it wasn't easy—and smoothed her skirts back over her crossed knees for her as he said, "So be it. I'm sorry I got so forward, Miss Consuela. Must be that romantic smelter glow and the rancid smell of yon babbling brook. What say I just carry you home, and we say no more about it?"

As he rose to help her to her considerable height, the gigantic widow demanded in a confounded voice if he really meant that.

He said, "Hardly ever say anything I don't mean to a lady. I don't know what you might have heard about *el Brazo Largo* from down Mexico way, but I've heard some of the Denver gossip about me around the federal building, so I can imagine. Don't you reckon we'd better be getting on back, before your reputation gets ruined forever?"

As he led her back along the cinder path, she said, "Nobody from Santa Fe is staying at our hotel. Do you always give up that easily?"

He said, "Have to. I'm bigger and stronger than some men, and you ladies are so inclined to put unwelcome persistance down as rape."

She softly asked him "Did I say your advances back there were so *unwelcome*, Custis?"

He shrugged and replied, "Not 'til I made a practical suggestion. We're both experienced adults, Miss Consuela. If I wanted to play kid games in a public park I'd find myself a kid."

She called him a brute and commenced to sniffle. He put an arm around her waist and got them to walking synchronized with their hips together at nigh the same level, soothing, "Don't cloud up and rain all over me, Miss Consuela. I meant I didn't *want* a silly young gal rolling around on the green grass with me where somebody might come along any time and occasion more trouble than the game is worth."

She pouted, "Is that all it is to you, a game, *el Brazo*

Largo? I've heard about you and those rebel girls, down Mexico way!"

He said, "Not from me. As for what you call it, in mixed company, I have to allow that English lord was right when he described careless slap and tickle as a fleeting pleasure at an exorbitant cost in a ridiculous position. That's how come I suggested we might finish what I thought we'd started behind a locked door back at our hotel. But since you won't go for that, and I ain't about to behave like a horny schoolboy on the village green, let's forget I ever offered such a shocking suggestion."

She fell silent for a spell. They hadn't walked far before she'd wanted to stop, so it didn't take long to get back to the hotel. As experienced travelers they'd both held on to their own room keys and had no call to pester the desk clerk. He, in turn, had no call to pester paid-up guests who didn't want anything.

He walked the Widow Garson past his door to her own and didn't wait for her to put her key in the lock before he thanked her for a swell evening and turned away.

She said, "Wait, Custis! I said I couldn't go to your room with you. I never said you might not be welcome in *mine*, did I?"

He turned to her with a wistful smile to reply, "You might have been right in the first place, ma'am. Seeing we've both had time to cool down a mite, it might be just as well if we called it a draw and left all the checkers on the board."

She pleaded, "For heaven's sake, let's not argue about it out here in the hall, you big goof!"

So he warily followed her in, silently cussing his own weak nature, for he'd meant what he'd just said.

She knew it. Women always seemed to. She moved closer to shut the hall door with her well padded chest against his own as he tried to to warn her, "Miss Consuela, I told you I was down here from Denver on a field mission. I told you there was no saying how long I'd be down this way. Come morning I'll be riding out to interview former pals of that escaped prisoner, and there's just no saying whether I'll be back this way some more or pressing on most any direction."

She leaned even closer, murmuring, "Custis . . ."

He said, "I ain't finished. I told you not to believe all that guff about *el Brazo Largo*, but a heap of it seems to have been the results of the more romantic Mexican approach to . . . romance."

She said, "Custis, I'm not Mexican, I'm land grant Spanish."

He said, "Whatever. The point I'm trying to make is that no matter what you are, I'm a natural born tumbleweed on a roving assignment. I eat, drink and enjoy other pleasures at such times as they don't get in the way of my job. My job comes first. It has to come first. Sometimes that makes *me* want to cry, too, but that's the way things have to be, and I've no right to mess with quality gals raised more delicate than me, so . . ."

Then she was between him and the door, albeit with both hands behind her as she got to work on those buttons, boldly stating, "I've told you about my all-too-brief, happy marriage, Custis. My husband was a big laconic Anglo, too. It takes a big man to satisfy a woman my size, and he used to say I went on too much about locking all the doors and trimming all the lamps. He teased I was more shy about my big old tits and ass than the sight of his you-know-what in broad daylight!"

Longarm gulped and tried, "Miss Consuela, mebbe . . ."

And then she was shucking her dress off over her head and there certainly was a heap of her to see by the street light lancing redly in through her window panes. Parlor house madams knew what they were about when they lit those ruby glass lamps to display their wares!

As Longarm could only watch, bemused, the looming

94

statuesque brunette tossed her summer dress aside and reached up to unpin her long black hair, and that was a wonderous sight to behold as she stepped around him toward the bed, murmuring, "Don't be shy, Custis. What are you still doing with your hat and gun belt on, you big silly?"

Then she'd spread herself across her bedstead, and there sure was a lot of woman to work with, there, softly molded by red light and purple shade as Longarm fumbled with his buckle, wondering where he ought to begin such a chore.

Chapter 11

Like most women, Consuela Garson was slower than most women to warm up and more than one man could ever completely satisfy, once they got started. But a man could try, and she did allow he was hung as well as she'd been hoping, once he had it in and they were going at it serious, with her doing more than half the work under him. Thanks to that long restful train ride and a warm meal since, Longarm felt too relaxed to hold until she came. But he was enough of a sport to leave it in her as she went on bucking. He'd thought she hadn't noticed until she crooned, "Oh, how sweet of you, darling! I think I'm almost there, too, and . . . Yes, yes, yessss!"

So, naturally, by that time he was fully erect again and ready to go on, that gigantic rump thrust up to encourage his dog style enthusiasm. It sure looked encouraging, glowing like a blushing ghost in the ruddy skylight of a Pueblo evening.

They naturally finished in a more romantic position, against one wall as he explored the possibilities of her astounding legs. Women liked wall jobs because of the way they felt a man's shaft against their clits in that position. But most men found the position a tad awkward because of the way they usually had to spread their own feet or bend their knees. Tall men like Longarm found the position downright tedious with a woman of average height, but with a lady giant with longer legs than his own, the results were delightful.

She said she liked it, too.

Then they got back in bed to share a smoke and allow their hearts to slow down. Over in the creekside park, Consuela had mentioned her husband dying young of a heart stroke. Longarm was beginning to see how such a calamity could occur around Consuela.

But he made it through the night alive and despite his earlier plans for an early start, he had to be a good sport about having a late breakfast with her on the American plan before they parted for the day to pursue their own chores.

Consuela said she had to have lunch with a contract wagon master. Longarm toted his saddle to the nearest livery on Main Street, with his Winchester and all, to hire a cordovan mare with a white blaze and Morgan lines at the steep big city rates of four bits a day.

Out on the trail, the mare seemed willing, or dispirited enough to carry him at an uncomfortable but mile-eating trot as he tried to make up for lost time.

The spread Crimp Gooding had bought with blood money lay well east of Fountain Creek and the city limits beyond, off the service road that followed the Arkansas River and railroad line running east to Wichita. They'd told him to watch for an antelope skull on the crossbar above the gateposts.

The prairie pronghorn was not, in fact, a real antelope, but it was hard to hit and getting scarce. So the old breed who'd sold out to Crimp Gooding and his own lumbago had been proud he'd shot whatever he'd shot and nailed it over his gate for all to admire as it sun-bleached.

Longarm didn't care. It would help him find the right

place, and a pronghorn skull over a gate seemed more civilized than that human skull they had above that bar in Bodie, out California way.

As he'd hoped, Longarm spied a pinpoint of chalk white above a distant roadside gate long before they trotted over to it. He had to dismount to open the counterweighted gate; horse spreads couldn't rely on cattle guards.

Longarm led his mount afoot, and the office cum quarters at one end of the long rambling complex of low-roofed frame structures erected and painted various shades of barn red on different occasions had a whitewashed dutch door with the top flap open.

So the gal inside had seen him opening that gate, and, as he led his livery nag nearer, she darted out of the house barefoot in her shimmy shirt to fall to her knees before him, imploring, "Please don't kill me! I didn't know they were going go to it! They made me testify in court like so! They said they'd shoot my dog and drown my mother if I refused to go along with them!"

Her red hair was no more real red hair than that antelope skull was a real antelope skull. But after that, she was almost pretty and built even better. So he figured it was just as well he'd torn off that friendly wake-up piece in even nicer surroundings, back at the hotel.

He said, "I ain't a friend of the Fargo Kid's, Miss Trixie. I'm the law, federal, sent down this way to save Crimp Gooding for the War Department by running Fargo in before he can make good on his threats, see?"

She did. Leaping to her feet, she came closer to wrap both arms around his waist and bury her henna-rinsed head in the loose folds of his tweed frock coat as she sobbed, "Oh, praise the Lord! I've been so scared, all alone out here like this after hearing Fargo's new pals cut those other lawmen up just awful!"

She was an outlaw's leavings who needed a bath, and

he was still glad he'd just had some, thank you very much. For he suspected most men would fuck a dung heap if they had a hard-on and the dung heap wasn't putting up a fight.

She suggested they go inside lest one of those mysterious pals of the Fargo Kid pick them off with a long-range buffalo gun. So he asked the way to the nearest horse trough, and she led him and the cordovan around to the stable yard where he could tether the mare in shade with water at her disposal. She thanked them by pissing a lot as the two of them headed for a back door across the yard.

In her untidy kitchen, Trixie Davis sat Longarm down and served him spit-warm coffee and stale store-bought sponge cake, but at least she was trying, so he addressed her friendly as he asked where Crimp Gooding might be.

She said Crimp had lit out right after they'd gotten that death threat from the Fargo Kid. She added, "Crimp has every right to be scared. It was *his* grand notion to turn Fargo in, and the Kid has always been dangerous to cross!"

Longarm nibbled just enough stale cake to be polite before he asked where they thought Gooding could have gone.

She sat down across from him, oblivious to how much of her curves were obvious under that thin sateen chemise as she said, "Mel said Crimp had mentioned having other pals in Leadville, up the river and around a big bend behind the Front Range. I don't know where *Mel's* gone! He ran out on me and left me to fend for myself alone, after I was so good to him, too!"

Longarm suggested, not unkindly, "You know what they say about men, Miss Trixie. I know it ain't fair. Men and women both deserve something better than one another, but there you have it. How come you're still here if you're so scared?"

She sobbed, "You don't *know* how scared I am! I don't have words to describe it! But where would I go if I didn't wait here for Mel and Crimp to come back?"

He told her, firmly, "They ain't coming back. Take the word of yet another love-'em-and-leave-'em polecat, Miss Trixie. With all due respect to what must have started out pure and innocent, had either of them really cared about your continued existence, they'd have taken you along as they lit out. I owe you for that lead on Leadville. So could you use some fatherly advice?"

She sobbed, "My father was a drunken brute. He raped me when I was eight and sold my favors for drinking money shortly thereafter."

Longarm said, "I'll just advise you as a ship passing friendly in the night, then. The first thing you ought to do would be to run, not walk, clean out of Colorado. Go east, young woman, and lose yourself in a crowded city. Then, change your hair to another color entire and move to yet *another* big city under another new name. We figure Frank and Jesse have done something like that, and we're better at hunting folk down that your average revenge killer."

She said, "Maybe you're right. Maybe I could sell this place, and the stock out back for enough to start over with someone who'd watch over me better!"

He shook his head and said, "If you have the time for a real estate deal and even casual horse trading, the Fargo Kid ain't really coming. I read somewhere how tropical natives trap monkey paws by drilling a modest hole in a coconut shell and dropping some peanuts inside. When a monky smells the peanuts, he finds he can just slip his paw inside. When he shuts his fist around a pawful of peanuts, he finds he can't get his fist out. But, being a monkey, he's too dumb to let go, and so he's still stuck there, trying to pull that fistful of peanuts out when they come to put him in the cage, or cooking pot."

He let that sink in before he soberly added, "Just let go and *run* for it, Miss Trixie. I can tell 'em in town there's nobody out this way to tend the stock and the county will doubtless be proud to take over. You'll be no more out-of-pocket than you were before Gooding bought this spread with money you never earned and . . ."

"A lot *you* know!" she cut in, blurting, "I had to fuck them both, and then they made me appear in court against the man who'd really cared for me, and what-oh-what would you have me *do* in some big city to support myself until I can find some other man to watch over me?"

He said, "Working in a halfway tidy parlor house won't hurt no worse than being passed around by uncaring outlaws along the owlhoot trail, Miss Trixie. As for that mythical man who's going to watch over you in the sweet by-and-by, when all your other dreams come true, allow me to pass on the advice of Madam Ruth Jacobs, Madam Emma Gould and some other . . . women of experience I've met up with, in the line of duty."

She smirked, "I've heard of those two famous Denver whores. So which one of them screws best?"

He sternly replied, "I said I'd *jawed* with them in the line of duty. I mean to interview some other Madams when I get to Leadville. They can be a fount of information about new faces in town. The advice I feel sure any older whore would give one young as yourself involves that man who's going to watch over you in your dreams, Miss Trixie. There ain't no such animal. A man of any substance who'd marry up with a . . . soiled dove, is a man who needs someone to watch over *him*! I know gals who've never been passed around that much who've long since made up their mind nobody with a lick of gumption *needs* anybody watching over 'em. Get yourself safely away, change your name and general outline and get some money set aside before you even consider a serious understanding with another man. No offense, but like many a know-it-all rider of the owlhoot trail, Miss Trixie, you're a born sucker!"

Meanwhile, back in town, Deputy Roy Manx and Increase Younger were staring at one another in wonder as she let him in through her kitchen door. She asked him what had possessed him to turn up at high noon on a workday.

He said, "We got to talk about that. What have you done to your hair, Creasy?"

She ran her fingers absently through the ash-blond tresses hanging down the front of her half-open kimono as she asked with a smile, "Do you like my natural hair color, Roy? I just finished rinsing out the last of that vegetable stain. I fear I've other little sins to confess to you, now that we've become . . . so close. But tell me what you're doing here at this hour, first."

He said, "It's my lunch hour. I can likely get away with more than a full hour if I say I was checking something out on my way back to the office. You know what I'm *here* for, Lord love you, but that pesky woman I just can't leave for the sake of my children has started to act suspicious about my getting home a little late of late."

She shut the door and took him by the hand to lead him to his fate in her bedroom as she purred, "We wouldn't want your wife to suspect you were getting any on the side, now, would we? But what am *I* to do for fun after sundown, alone in this big house with not even a friendly pup to lick my lonely privates!"

He gallantly suggested he meant to leave her satisfied for the day and night to follow. She assured him he was just awful, secretly delighted by this latest developement. For this way she'd have more free time after dark, and she hadn't been planning on showing herself and her new hairdo in broad day just yet.

So they got right to it, down and dirty sixty-nine, the way married men with prim and proper wives at home hungered for, and after she'd spit and lit a smoke to get rid of the taste, she told him, as he went on nibbling a big tit like a babe atop its comforting momma, "I've a naughty little secret to confide, Roy. You know how I told you I was a recent widow, looking to open a hat shop here in Pueblo with my late husband's insurance money? Well, that was just a lie. I've never been married."

He kissed her nipple and said, "That's good to hear, albeit, no offense, you surely fuck like a woman of such experience, Creasy."

She grimly replied, "I was broken in early by an expert. A . . . man I've never gotten over. But he's no longer with us, and I was never sent to prison as a whore, if that's what you're worried about!"

He raised his face from her chest to smile uncertainly and reply, "I wasn't worried about nothing, up to now. How come you were sent to prison, Creasy? How long, how come, and where were they holding you?"

She said, "I'm not sure I'm ready to tell you everything, yet. I only wanted to know whether we'd . . . still be friends if you found out I was an ex-convict."

He asked if she'd escaped or been set free. When she said she'd served her time she added, "All of it. I fear I resented prison life too much to abide by all their fussy rules. But I'm not wanted anywhere, if that's what you're worried about."

He kissed her tit some more, growling, "That's all I was worried about. About *you*, least ways. I never took you for an innocent Little Bo Peep, no offense. But God help me if my *wife* finds out about us!"

Chapter 12

The Fargo Kid could see that unlike his treacherous Trixie, the waitress he was buttering up in Denver's Parthenon Saloon was a natural redhead. He tried not to let his true feelings show as he asked in a desperately casual tone whether his pal, Longarm, had been in that afternoon. The son of a bitch hadn't been at the Black Cat the night before, so where in blue blazes *was* he?

The redhead at the Parthenon was commencing to cotton to the kid. He sure tipped well for a sport who didn't ask what time a girl got off. She truthfully told him, "Haven't seen him since yesterday or the day before. I can't say as I keep track of customers who don't give me any trouble. You say Custis is a pal of yours? Why don't you just ask for him at the nearby federal building? You know where he works over yonder, don't you?"

The Fargo Kid soberly assured her, "Sure I do. I already asked at the marshal's office. They said he was likely enjoying your free lunch, over here."

The waitress glanced down at the deviled eggs and cold cuts at the far end of the bar to reply, "Lord knows that tall drink of water can put pickled pig's feet away, albeit he's a sport about ordering draft needled with hard stuff we can charge him more than a nickel for. I see your own schooner's about empty, ah . . . I didn't catch the name, in case Custis comes in."

The Fargo Kid gave the name of a neighbor boy he'd never liked as a child. The ugly shit had been killed in the war, to be long forgotten as any possible associate. He declined her offer of a refill on the house and allowed he'd try that rooming house on the far side of Cherry Creek. He left a dime by his empty beer schooner. The redhead called after him, advising him not to be a stranger. Shy little riders who tipped generous and didn't pester an honest working girl were worth cultivating.

The Fargo Kid headed west afoot, considering his options as he made his way through the bustle of the Mile High City toward the Larimer Street bridge. He'd lied to the redhead about asking around the big marble federal building. Creasy had told him about Longarm shooting her gunslick brother on a marble staircase. They'd told him at the Black Cat the night before that if Longarm wasn't out of town on yet some other mission, he'd be getting off work at the federal building and heading home to spruce up before he searched for further action.

The Fargo Kid had pretended he knew the address of his target's rooming house. He had no plan for calling on Longarm at home. For a dumb stunt like that could take fifty years off a man's life. He had to get the drop on Longarm from behind, without the dangerous lawman suspecting shit. Knowing Longarm didn't know him on sight, the Fargo Kid meant to just stand there grinning like an innocent big ass bird until he could throw down on Longarm's back.

He had the advantage of knowing what Longarm looked like. Finding out had been duck soup simple. He'd traipsed over to the nearest newspaper office, told some whopping lies, and been allowed to look through their newspaper morgue until he found a line cut, traced from

106

a photograph, of Denver's own answer to Wild Bill Hickok. Whether it was an exact likeness or not, how many gents looking at all like so were going to be headed home across the Larimer Street bridge that evening in a tobacco tweed outfit, a coffee-brown Stetson porkpied Colorado style and standing a head taller than most, despite low-heeled cavalry stovepipe boots?

The stroll from the Parthenon down to Larimer Street and then south to where it passed a big amusement arcade to cross Cherry Creek by way of that wrought iron bridge took a spell as he window-shopped along the way, knowing he had time to kill. Some of those window dummies at the Denver Dry Goods department store sure looked sissy in those fancy summer suits and derby hats. It hardly seemed fair they should all be taller than him. Shorter gents bought derby hats as well, dammit, and shorter gents had feelings, too.

The Fargo Kid smiled thinly as he recalled that big husky bank guard, and how his sneering expression had changed to one of awed respect as he found himself staring down the muzzle of that good old Starr .44!

The Fargo Kid missed that old double-action pissoliver who'd ridden through thick and thin with him. The sons of bitches who'd arrested him had taken his away and, back in Pueblo, Creasy had been unable to replace it for him.

She'd told him, and he knew it was true, the Starr Arms Company of New York City had gone bust and out of business after producing only twenty thousand or so double-action .44s nigh a generation ahead of a ready market for such an expensive sidearm.

On sale in time for a war with the powerful and popular Colt Dragoon selling for $17.50 apiece, the more advanced but less famous Starr had cost its makers money when they offered it at $15.25, or a tad less than it had cost to make. But that was ancient history to the Fargo

Kid, for the designers of both the Starr double-action and the bodacious Colt Dragoon were dead, and he'd had to settle for the Colt double-action .41 Thunderer Model she'd bought him, saying any six-gun good enough for John Wesley Hardin had to good enough for the likes of *him*, the sarcasticated bitch!

He was packing his new gun concealed in a shoulder rig that afternoon, Denver having a municipal ordinance about wearing guns to town. Hardin had packed the same model in his own shoulder rig up to the time they'd caught him. The Fargo Kid suspected some of Hardin's rep as a quick draw artist stemmed from his packing a double-action under his coat in a shoulder rig. A man needed every edge he could manage in a shoot-out.

Arriving at the bridge with time to spare, the Fargo Kid circled aimlessly, scouting for the best position to back-shoot a taller man headed south across Cherry Creek. Leaning on the rail as if waiting for someone else offered an easy shot at his chosen target's back, but then what? He had to get out of sight, pronto, before the Denver P.D. responded to gunshots in downtown Denver during the evening rush hour!

He moseyed over to the Larimer Street Arcade and drifted as if only killing time through the maze of penny machines, candy-apple stands and street drifters trying not to look interested in him as he scouted for a back exit. When a shabby youth in a plug hat siddled up to ask if he was looking for boys or girls, the Fargo Kid said he preferred sheep and moved back to the sunlit street, deciding against *that* escape route. It hardly mattered which way you ran if you left a trail of eyeballs and pointing fingers after you.

He walked slowly across the bridge to see the sidewalks end and Larimer Street continue as a welter of wagon ruts across an ad hoc pavement of cinders, dry horseshit and the adobe soil of the High Plains. Hard as plaster in dry weather but gumbo, threatening to suck your boots off, when wet.

This might be the place, the Fargo Kid thought as he strolled by some more humble neighborhood shops and the verandas of run-down frame houses. He turned up a narrow side lane as an experiment. A yard dog barked and a back door opened. He said, "Shit!" and moved back to the more traveled way to retrace his path back across the bridge as he decided, "This shapes up to be too big a boo. But what if we were to just follow him home after work and wait for him to come back out to go roaming in the gloaming? Who'd be certain what they were seeing if he got hit from behind crossing this bridge *towards* the bright lights?"

He crossed over to buy a tamale and a bottle of orange pop from a street vendor before he leaned against the bridge rail with an excuse for being there.

It wouldn't be long, now, and, dammit, he *wasn't* spooked. He was only feeling . . . cautious, as a man had every right to feel when fixing to gun another man of any rep. As he washed down some spicy cornmeal with sickly sweet pop, he assured himself it didn't matter how fast a man might be on the draw if you never gave him the chance to draw at all. It didn't matter how good a shot a man was if you shot him first within less than say five yards. Increase had warned and he'd felt no call to argue that *missing* a gunslick like Longarm with your first shot could be injurious to your health as putting gunpowder in your pipe to see if you could smoke it.

"If I had a lick of sense," he told his hot tamale, "I'd haul out of here and not bet my ass in a feud I never pledged it to! Longarm ain't after me! He's never done shit to me or mine! There's no bad blood betwixt us, and they say he moves like spit on a hot stove and busts nine bottles out of ten at fifty yards. With a fucking *pistol*!"

But he knew Increase Younger would never move on

his real enemies before she read in the papers he'd done Longarm for her. So he seemed stuck with the deal, unless he was willing to extend his live-and-let-live feelings to Mel, Crimp and that two-timing Trixie!

He bit into the tamale some more and decided, "Don't want to let even *one* of them live. Want all three of them dead! So what in the fuck am I doing all the way up here in Denver, set to gun a man I've never met, when the three buckets of shit I'm really after are gathered down Pueblo way?"

Down Pueblo way, Longarm's mind was running in the same channels as he strode not towards his furnished digs up in Denver but toward that hotel after searching in vain for a better lead on the elusive Crimp Gooding. He didn't really give a shit where Mel Stuart might be at the moment.

Consuela Garson had likely been watching from her upstairs window. For she met him in the lobby wearing a fresh frock she'd just unpacked or bought. When you were rich you didn't have to wear wilted duds in summertime. He'd left his saddle upstairs earlier to go chasing all over town. So he agreed an early supper might be in order and stole a feel in the archway betwixt the lobby and the hotel dining room.

The blue plate that evening was fresh venison down from the front range. They'd been talking about a restricted hunting season since the die-off of the northern buffalo herd had worried some folk. But they'd never pass that fool notion about an income tax, neither, unless the world changed a heap.

As they waited for the venison, he asked if she'd ever had any pronghorn. She said she doubted it and asked if it was good as deer meat. He shook his head and explained, "I was minded of pronghorn, earlier today, out at that stud spread I told you about. I'd have to be mighty hungry to shoot another. Where they ain't muscle, tough

110

enough to run faster than a locomotive, antelope seem to be all *lung*. Shoot one broadside, and four out of five times the bullet will pass through the rib cage from side to side without hitting anything but antelope breath. They tend to drop later from infection, of course, but a lung-shot antelope can run clean over the horizon whilst you're wondering how you could have missed!"

She sighed and asked, "Custis, why do you keep bringing up the subject of *blood* at suppertime?"

He smiled sheepishly and explained, "Just thinking back to other futile hunting trips. I've wired Leadville as well as Denver about it being possible Crimp Gooding headed up that way. But the more I study on it, the more I wonder whether the spooked sneak stopped anywheres that close. He surely knows that when your pals figure you might have gone on up to Leadville a *former* pal sworn to clean your plow might figure you've gone on up to Leadville."

Consuela made a wry face and replied, "If you say so, *querido*. But why would *anybody* want to go to Leadville? I've been there, once, and once was enough."

He smiled indulgently and suggested, "That's likely because you ain't a gold digger."

She asked, "Do they dig *gold* in a town called *Leadville*?"

He said, "Not directly. The mother lode is lead carbonate tainted with as much as forty ounces of silver a ton. They named the strike Leadville instead of Silverton to discourage the real gold diggers, the whores and gamblers who buzz around mines the way flies tend to buzz around . . . stables."

She said, "Thank you. Here comes our soup."

The soup du jour was split pea that night. The venison and home fries with string beans to follow was better. So they didn't get back on the subject of Leadville until they were having dessert, which was cherry pie, wild choke cherries with heaps of sugar and a long spell in the oven. Black coffee made it seem sweeter than the cook had been able to manage out back.

He explained how Crimp Gooding, having lost his ill-gotten gains he'd tied up in property he couldn't ride off with at full gallop, had a renewed interest in sudden wealth. "Cutting a prosperous mining man out of the herd and robbing him at gunpoint in an alley has to sound easier than sticking up a bank or stopping a train all by yourself. That poor scared Trixie I told you about thinks a second pal, Mel Stuart, may have headed up that way to join Crimp. Two such worthless skunks add up to more serious plans and . . ."

"Did you make love to her?" Consuela cut in.

Longarm looked insulted and replied with indignation, "Great day in the morning, don't you credit me with any delicacy at all? Had you ever seen her you'd take my word I never even held hands with her!"

To which Consuela sweetly replied, "I've never seen her. So we'll just have to take you right upstairs and find out whether you've fired that weapon into anyone else this afternoon, won't we?"

Chapter 13

Having satisfied herself in more ways than one, Consuela wanted Longarm to see her home to Santa Fe in the morning and acted sort of miffed when he allowed he couldn't. So when she refused to have her breakfast with him, Longarm ambled over to the Western Union to see if they'd let him come home yet.

They wouldn't. Billy Vail's night letter warned some person or persons unknown had been asking about Longarm around the Parthenon, the Black Cat and even the corner fruit stand near his rooming house. Vail suggested that whilst he had Deputies Smiley and Dutch out looking for the sneaky bastards, Longarm might as well mosey on up to Leadville and see if he could locate Crimp Gooding.

Longarm had already wired that he only had an unbacked rumor to go by, since their pals with the Lake County Sheriff's Department had wired back they'd never heard of the son of a bitch.

But since Billy wanted him to give Leadville a shot, and since Consuela had stormed out of Pueblo describing him as an unfeeling brute, he checked out. Longarm then toted his shit to the narrow-gauge loading platform and bought a one-way from Pueblo to Leadville, seeing he'd be heading over to Denver by way of a shorter local line, Lord willing and he didn't run into that big blond gal out to kill him.

He though about that, a heap, as he rode the narrow gauge alongside the brawling upper Arkansas that morning. For if they knew at the federal building he was headed for Leadville, the spies of old Increase Younger might know.

She had to be working with spies. His own pals around Denver would have said so if a six-foot-six woman with any color hair had been asking where he was. An outlaw's sister who'd done ten at hard in her own right would have surely met a mess of other crooks of all shapes and sizes by this late in the game. Billy Vail would be trying to play it close to his vest, but they couldn't count on nobody blabbing, and *he* couldn't count on spotting a freakishly tall woman in time if she had more human looking sidekicks backing her play!

"I should have gone back to Santa Fe with Consuela and run her freight line for her, as she pleaded, dog style," he softly muttered as he dug out a cheroot.

"I beg your pardon?" asked the mousy-at-first-glance gal seated just behind him, alone in her own unpadded seat to one side of the narrow gauger's off-center side aisle.

On second glance she wasn't bad, despite her specs and straight hair the color of weak tea. So he said, "I was asking if you minded did I smoke in your presence, ma'am."

She got prettier as she dimpled and said, "For heaven's sake, the windows are open, and nothing you could possibly smoke could smell worse than that diamond stacker just ahead of us!"

"That's why I was fixing to light this cheroot," he lied, adding he had others he could spare if she cared to join him.

She blushed becomingly and said she wasn't one of those women, even if she was headed up to Leadville.

Longarm didn't care. Billy Vail hadn't ordered him up to Leadville to get laid. Even if Billy had, they'd be getting there at an awkward hour, and she'd just said she wasn't that kind of women. He had no call to ask he what kind of woman she was, but he was stuck aboard the same cranky, twisty narrow gauge for an all-day trip through dramatic scenery at a tedious pace.

The infernal dinky train kept stopping every few miles like a pokey stagecoach, albeit they kept taking on boiler water instead of changing teams. There was no dining car, of course, and when they stopped for dinner at Salida, they were told to get off and take half an hour, no more, no less, grubbing up at the trackside diner.

By that time, whether he'd wanted to or not, Longarm had found out she was a Miss Rowena Burnes, who'd always been good with figures. So she'd been hired by a "Winc Theater" on State Street to keep the books.

She waited until he'd sprung for her noon dinner, having little other choice, before she shyly asked if he knew what a wine theater was.

He suggested they polish off their chili con carne with oyster crackers, first, lest they wind up marooned in Salida, and saucered her hot coffee for her so's she could wash her chili down before they ran back to the train.

Once they were under way again he explained how most of the variety theaters along State Street charge no admission but posted signs that openly stated patrons who didn't patronize the bar would be asked to leave. He didn't add that when you were asked to leave a Leadville wine theatre you damn well *left* if you knew what was good for you. She'd find out what the brawling mining camp was like ere long and then she'd either fit in or leave aboard this same narrow-gauge line. Professor Darwin, over in England, described the process of western expansion as *evolution*.

Not being Chinee, Rowena Burnes was likely in no serious danger. They hardly ever threw anyone but Chinee down abandoned mine shafts up Leadville way. That had something to do with the hardrock miner's union. They weren't allowed by the owners to have a union, but they had one, anyhow, and posted other signs openly stating that anybody hiring or working as "coolie labor" would be kangarooed, with the burden of proof falling on anybody who might possibly be a coolie.

She found it more reassuring to be told they were commencing to get up-to-date in Leadville, what with Silver Dollar Tabor and his grim but kind-hearted Miss Augusta endowing the town with a spanking new opera house and a marching band of Highland pipers.

She said she'd heard Horace Tabor lived over in Denver with a mistress young enough to be his daughter.

Longarm grimaced and warned her, "Don't ask about that once we get to Leadville, Miss Rowena. The young woman of whom you speak, a Miss Baby Doe, is still married up to her Mister Doe, and Silver Dollar Tabor is still officiously residing in both Leadville and a swell new mansion on Sherman Street in Denver with his formidable wife of lo these many years. Some say it's thanks to Miss Augusta that old Horace Tabor went from a general store proprietor to a silver baron almost overnight. *He* was willing to *trust* prospectors for camp supplies. It was his wife who made them sign away shares in any color they struck in exchange for credit."

"Then why has he been cheating on her with that horrid Baby Doe?" she asked. Women always seemed confused by such developments.

Longarm patiently explained, "Baby Doe ain't horrid, Miss Rowena. I have examined both specimens at a discreet distance. So I can tell you Miss Baby Doe is pretty as a picture and smart as a brick. Her Mr. Doe ain't much brighter and has a drinking problem. Some say, but don't ever ask about this up Leadville way, old Silver Dollar Tabor bailed Harvey Doe out of a jam involving a Denver house of ill repute. The deal called for Doe to leave town, and Baby's divorce from him ought to be final any day now."

Rowena asked, "What about poor Augusta and could any grown woman really be named *Baby*?"

Longarm said, "Her real name may be Elizabeth. But nobody who's ever laid eyes on her calls her anything but Baby, and that's sort of complimenting her intelligence."

Before she could cloud up and rain on him he soothed, "As for Miss Augusta, Silver Dollar will take good care of her, if he knows as much about sheer survival as the average old goat with an eye for younger wives. *She's* likely as tired of *him*, by now, and once she gets her hands on a million or so to spend on her own, other gents are likely to decide she's *distinguished*. That's what plain folk with lots of money look like, distinguished. Some expect Horace Tabor to go broke sudden, less her brains, backing his razzle-dazzle style."

She asked him about Leadville in general. The conversation covering the three hundred tons of silver a year shipped by Leadville, not counting the lead, added up to dry statistics next to the scandal of Baby Doe and her Silver Dollar sugar daddy. But the born bookkeeper wanted 'em, so Longarm told her. The last time he'd counted, there'd been 19 hotels, 11 boarding houses, some of them really renting rooms, with 38 restaurants, 82 saloons, 21 gambling casinos and half a dozen fly-by-night wine theaters competing with the Grand Central and Horace Tabor's big new opera house.

The chaos was served by 7 smelters, 10 lumber yards, 12 blacksmiths and 3 undertakers. He didn't think she wanted to hear about the whorehouses but she seemed cheered to hear of the new Saint Vincent's hospital established by the Sisters of Mercy. He didn't mention the Irish volunteers who'd kicked the shit out of the land-grabbers who'd run the Presbyterians off *their* prime lot near the center of town. He'd been told things were calming down under a tough new marshal appointed by, who else, Mayor Tabor.

By the time they got in, close to sundown, they felt as if they'd been through a war together, and Longarm knew she didn't know anybody half so well in Leadville. But to his mild chagrin and considerable relief she was met at the D&RGRR terminal by a gent with a seersucker suit, a diamond tie stud and, more importantly, a buggy to carry the pretty little thing and her baggage out of Longarm's life.

It sure beat all how *pretty* gals got as one said *goodbye* to them in the soft light of gloaming.

He toted his own shit, on foot, to the Chrysolite on State Street, handy to the action, and stored it safely, or off his hands, least ways, before heading for the Western Union to tell Billy Vail where he was and ask if they'd found out where Increase Younger and her mysterious pals might be.

He didn't hire a flop on the American plan at the Chrysolite. He'd stayed there before. They changed the linen betwixt guests and the most noticable bugs were cockroaches. But they had no dining room, and, judging by the stale smell of last winter's soft coal and more recently chewed tobacco lingering in the lobby, that was likely just as well. So he found a Greek joint.

He treated himself to steak smothered in onions with a baked spud on the side, washed down a slab of serviceberry pie with passable coffee, and ambled over to the county courthouse betwixt Fifth and Sixth to pay a courtesy call on the Lake County Sheriff's Department and see if they had anything about Crimp Gooding for him.

They didn't. As usual, at that hour, he found the premises guarded by children, told the kid at the desk where he could be found, and went to the nearby marshal's office to repeat the process. He was again told their boss, the renowned town tamer, Mart Duggan, had left for the day. Longarm didn't care. Mart Duggan seemed all right. He'd tidied up the reign of terror resulting from the murder of a softer or less fortunate City Marshal O'Connor, killed in a drunken brawl by one of his own men, who was still running.

Aided in part by an ad hoc miner's vigilance committee, Duggan was reputed to have run more than a hundred troublemakers out of town, not counting Chinese nor Indians. But Longarm couldn't help feeling a certain disdain for a man who carved notches in his gun grips like a buscadero in a Ned Buntline yarn.

So once again he felt just as glad to have let it be known he was in town and then haul ass outside as the town started coming to life after supper.

He saw by torchlight how the Comique, Gaiety and New Theatres on State Street were advertising "The Female Bathers," "Shot in the Eye" or "Who Stole the Dog," provided you ordered a drink with your seat before curtain time. He'd never thought to ask which wine theater Rowena Burnes would be keeping the books for. He idly wondered why he was wondering about that, now.

He decided to try the new Silver Dollar Saloon, established by the silver baron of the same designation between Third and Fourth, with a one dollar ante. He figured a knock-around hairpin short on traveling money would be more interested in games of chance than female bathers or stolen dogs. He had a tight description but no personal recall as to what Crimp Gooding looked like. But that seemed fair. Old Crimp had no idea what *he* looked like and didn't know anybody but the Fargo Kid was looking for him.

It was early yet but the big saloon was already crowded and blue with tobacco smoke as Longarm entered, sizing the crowd up for any cuss above average height, broad across the beam, with black curly hair and eyebrows that met in the middle. Crimp might or might not be wearing a mustache of late. A knockaround rider on the dodge could be expected to dress most any way. But they said Crimp favored a Remington-Beals .44 with ivory grips, worn side-draw.

Unlike Denver, Leadville had no sidearms regulation, or Marshal Duggan chose not to push his luck. A sign above the Faro table by a back wall read, CARD CHEATS, PIMPS AND CHINAMEN! STRETCH YOUR LEGS AND GET OUT OF TOWN BEFORE WE STRETCH YOUR NECKS: VIGILANCE COMMITTEE.

The gal in a low-cut black velveteen ball gown dealing faro at the table with her back to the wall looked bored and listless as she tended her shoe without looking down at the cards. The four sports bucking the tiger on Longarm's side of the table were paying more attention to her than the cards she was dealing them. They had a point. She looked haughty and cold, but she was young and pretty, too, and doubtless had what they call a ring dang doo to go with her pinned up chestnut hair and copper penny eyes. One of the men with his back to Longarm was thickset, dressed cow, and the six-gun that Longarm was trying to get a better look at was worn low with ivory grips.

So Longarm moseyed over, and, despite her blasé bluff the faro-dealing gal wasn't missing much as another prospective sucker was moving in to join the fun.

She looked sort of familiar, as if they'd brushed by somewhere long ago and far away. He didn't know she'd recognized him as well until she suddenly blurted, "Longarm! Behind you!"

He spun, as most men would have, to see a shorter,

somewhat older man he recognized at a glance had seen him first and already slapped leather!

A single shot rang out.

Then it got very quiet in the Silver Dollar Saloon as the other man stared owl-eyed at Longarm through the gunsmoke hanging in the air betwixt them as Longarm held his fire, calmly saying, "Evening, Mr. Sinclair. Long time no see."

The seriously wanted Fuzzy Sinclair croaked, "How . . . did . . . you . . . do . . . that?" before his knees crumpled and he fell at Longarm's feet, dead as a turd in a milk bucket.

Chapter 14

As a low but ominous rumble broke the silence the faro-dealing gal now facing Longarm's back called out, "It's all right, boys, the winner's the law!"

But the crowd still rumbled some as one of the bouncers and a man dressed like an undertaker with a badge pinned to his lapel moved in to loom just the other side of the figure oozing into the sawdust on the floor. So Longarm reloaded his derringer, declaring for any and all to hear, "His name was Melvin aka Fuzzy Sinclair. Road agent and bank robber. Wanted federal for a couple of post office jobs and the untimely death of an Indian agent out Tucson way."

The Leadville lawman said, "I'll take your word for that. Others say you had that derringer palmed in your hand when you walked in off Fourth Street just now. You mind telling us how come?"

Longarm glanced down as he put the belly gun away, saying, "That's how come. He wasn't the want I'm in town in search of, but are *you* in the habit of entering a lion's dens unprepared?"

The Silver Dollar's bouncer complained, "Watch what

you're calling a lion's den, stranger! We try to run a respectable place here!"

The girl behind Longarm trilled helpfully, "He's not a
stranger, Frank. He's that federal deputy you've doubtless
read about in the *Rocky Mountain News*. They call him
Longarm and that son of a bitch he just shot was fixing
to shoot him in the back!"

The town law, who seemed to be called Pappy in spite
of looking younger than Longarm, hunkered down to go
through the dead man's pockets as he grudgingly observed, "I read the papers. Is it fair for a gent with a rep
as a pistoleer to surprise folk like that with a derringer?"

Longarm didn't think such a stupid question deserved
an answer. So it was Frank the bouncer who observed,
"Rita says the loser was out to shoot him in the back,
Pappy!"

Pappy opened a wallet he'd found to remark, "This
Pueblo voter's registration card don't give his name as
Fuzzy Sinclair. Says here he was a Democrat named Stu-
art, Melvin Stuart."

Longarm had to study on that before he decided, "Sure
is a small world. I was looking for a Mel Stuart, *too*!
Didn't know he was a federal want, but *he* knew he was,
recognized me from back when I'd arrested him summer
before last, and thus we've resolved what just happened."

He raised his voice to be heard all the way to the front
as he announced, "If anyone in the crowd is Crimp Gooding, I didn't shoot your pal just now because we were at
feud. I've come to Leadville to save your hide if you'd
care to come forward."

Nobody did. Getting back to his feet, Pappy suggested,
"Maybe the *second* one changed his name recent for business reasons. What do you want with him if you ain't out
to arrest him?"

Longarm snapped the derringer back on his watch chain
and put it away as he replied, "Material witness, with

another killer on his trail. My orders are to find him first and carry him back to Denver."

The Leadville lawman said, "Not tonight you won't. We like to do things right in this Lake County. You're not to leave town before our coroner hears this case and allows you *can!*"

Longarm soothed, "Don't get yourself all sweaty, pard. I can't go home without Crimp Gooding and, as you see, he's not here or he's not willing to talk to me right now. I'm booked into the Chrysolite Hotel and your undertaker can bill this stiff to me once the county is done with the inquest. It's unfair as all get-out, but they make me pay the funeral expenses when I have to gun a suspect unless I can talk the local law into taking the stiff off my hands for the bounty I ain't allowed to put in for. But why am I telling another lawman all this? Could I buy you a drink as we wait on the meat wagon?"

Pappy said he didn't aim to get friendlier before he'd cleared it with his superiors. Longarm shrugged and turned away to thank the faro-dealing gal who'd just saved his bacon.

She said she didn't drink whilst dealing cards but suggested she might take him up on that when she got off at midnight, provided things were slow. She added, "When the boys are really bucking the tiger on a payday night I sometimes have to deal past dawn, and I do admire your palmistry, Longarm. Have you been hanging out with stage magicians or dishonest gamblers?"

He sheepishly replied "You've got sharp eyes, Miss . . . ?"

"Rita Malone, they call me Rio Rita," she dimpled with a mocking glance down at his big right hand still palming that derringer the others had thought they'd seen him put away.

He didn't ask how come she paid so much attention to the hands of other folk. A professional card dealer who didn't pay attention to everyone's hands was by definition not a professional dealer.

He told her he'd owe her that drink for now as he saw the morgue wagon crew moving in to gather up Fuzzy Sinclair. He followed Fuzzy out to the meat wagon and watched from the walk as it drove away. Then he turned to Frank and Pappy to ask if he was free to move it on down the pike, explaining he still had to find Crimp Gooding before the Fargo Kid could.

Pappy growled, "Jesus H. Christ, how many gunfighters did you bring to Leadville for us, Uncle Sam?"

Longarm shrugged and said, "Nary a one. I'm only here because I suspect at least two preceded me. Crimp Gooding was said to have left Pueblo for these parts. As Mel Stuart, the late Fuzzy Sinclair seems to have come looking for him. It remains to be seen whether Gooding or the man out to kill him, the Fargo Kid, are in or about Leadville. I don't know about you, but I eat an apple a bite at a time and try to avoid jumping at conclusions."

Pappy said he was free to go as long as he didn't jump aboard any trains until further notice. So they shook on it, and Longarm moved on, trying not to feel swell-headed about his sleight of hand as he shifted the derringer back to the palm he'd just shook with.

He'd read how the handshake had been invented in olden times to show gents you were meeting up with that you weren't packing any concealed weapon. He'd read how Sicilians and Scotch Highlanders had still managed serious daggers up their sleeves.

He went to the dance hall on State Street run by Belle Siddons under her new name, Madame Vestal. As Belle Siddons, she'd been a notorious whore cum Confederate spy. Under a new name more acceptable in a ferociously Union state, she was still a whore and her dance hall was vice den offering everything from sexual freak shows in a back room to most every game of chance a sport with money burning a hole in his pocket might fancy. They even had gals on the premises who'd dance with you, for a nominal fee.

He had better luck at Madame Vestal's as far as anyone slapping leather on him went. After that, nursing two and a half schooners of beer as he drifted, Longarm failed to spy anyone answering to the description of Crimp Gooding.

He knew for a fact who Gooding really was. Billy Vail had cut the blunty jumper's trail from that all-points on the Fargo Kid, and there was no doubt who the Fargo Kid was, if only someone would put out a good photograph of the mean little bastard.

"This is getting complexicated by half!" Longarm told himself as he moved on, and on, through one clip joint and card house after the other. But all he'd really learned by going on midnight was that he'd missed a sold-out performance of *Fra Diavalo* or "The Devil's Brother" at the opera house, speaking of daggers up sleeves.

He didn't care. A certain statuesque society widow had demanded to be escorted to the fool opera down Denver way, and he hadn't cared for it much, albeit some of the music had been all right.

As he headed back toward the Silver Dollar through the thinning crowd under a sullen red sky, Longarm found himself softly crooning

"On yonder rock reclining,
Diavalo waits, a gun in his hand!"

"Damn fool romantic twaddle!" Longarm growled as he thought back to the fuss he'd had with that otherwise attractive young widow as they rode home to her place after *Fra Diavalo*. Being he worked as a lawman, Longarm had a time understanding what was so romantic about outlaws. As he'd argued with that Denver fan of *Fra Dia-*

valo, there was no point in passing laws and paying gents to enforce 'em if it was so right and just to *break* 'em. He'd pointed out how men his size could likely take care of themselves in a world without laws if they just let women, children and puny little gents handle those romantic bandit chiefs as best they were able.

So Rio Rita asked what he was scowling about as he strode in to find her alone at her faro layout in the back.

He smiled sheepishly and confessed, "Feeling sorry for myself, I reckon. That jasper I came to town for doesn't seem to be in town, and now I can't leave. But I'd be proud to buy you that drink or anything else you'd like if I can fit it on my expense account. Saving the life of a federal employee rates something more than a simple thank-you!"

She said, "The last thing I could use after a night on my feet inhaling secondhand cigar smoke and beer fumes would be a belly-up to the bar. But I'd sure like it if you and that palmed derringer were to see me safely home at this hour. A barkeep named Bockhouse, Karl Bockhouse, was robbed as he came off shift not long ago. Karl killed one of the rascals, and Marshal Duggan caught the other. But I'm a girl."

So Longarm and his derringer walked her home. Her quarters were three long blocks west on Maple Street, above a dress shop closed for the night. She naturally invited him up for a nightcap, and they naturally wound up on her sofa with her feet propped higher over one arm of the same with her head in Longarm's lap as she declared that sure felt good. He assumed she meant propping her tired feet up like that. He doubted she could feel the stirrings in his lap, under her chestnut curls. She'd let her hair down, leading him up the stairs.

As he awkwardly slipped off his gun-rig to drape it over the other arm of the sofa lest she bruise her scalp on his .44-40. Rio Rita smiled up at him to say, "I'll rustle up that nightcap and mayhaps some scrambled eggs as soon as my feet can feel the floor again. I have tried dealing faro seated at the table, but it's awkward and it doesn't seem to please the customers as much."

He took off his hat and tossed it over the side without comment as he wondered whether it was too soon to bend over and kiss her. He knew she knew the effect that low-cut bodice had on mortal men while she willowed back and forth above her faro shoe. But for all he knew her feet were really hurting. So he just asked if she'd like him to rub them for her.

She gasped, "Oh, *would* you, ah . . . Custis? I haven't had a good foot massage in ages!"

He told her to let him up and swing her head down the other way. So she did and they wound up with her feet instead of her head in his lap as she reclined against the far arm of the sofa with her knees right high and damned if she had anything on under her black velveteen as far as he could tell.

He refrained from bending for a better look up under her skirts as he unbuttoned her high-heeled shoes. As he did so, she wondered aloud whether she ought to wash her feet before he touched them, explaining that she'd bathed and changed socks earlier but she'd been standing and sweating in those high-button shoes for an eternity.

He soothed, "Easier for me to wash my hands, after, as it would be to wash and dry these weary little feet before."

She started to cry quietly as he shucked her shoes and proceeded to shake hands with her feet, a foot in each hand as he half turned on the sofa to face her, forcing her knees up some for a better grasp of the situation.

She moaned, "Oh, Lord, that feels good! But be careful, Custis, I fear I'm not wearing any unmentionables under this skirt!"

He said, "I ain't afraid, and we just won't mention how a lady might or might not cope with the atmosphere of a stuffy saloon in summertime. Don't curl your toes under like that when your feet are tired. That's asking for a cramp."

She gasped, "Oh, Jesus! You warned me too late and it hurts like hell! The right one! For God's sake, let me stand up and stamp that stupid foot, Custis!"

He said he had a better way and let go of her left foot to hold her right ankle, grip her toes, and bend everything the other way until she sighed, "Ooooh! You just saved my life! Where did you ever learn to treat a woman so swell with those big strong hands, Custis?"

He said, "I was invited to this war they were giving, one time. You learn a heap about foot cramps marching fifty miles or more at a stretch. Once you learn how to bend your own toes right, I've yet to meet anyone, male or she-male, who's feet failed to cramp or uncramp about the same."

As he massaged both again he continued, "What we're trying for now is restored circulation. We'll talk later about your bad habit of standing in one place with locked knees."

She laughed and asked how he knew how her knees worked under her long black skirts.

He said, "Barkeeps, soldiers on sentry duty and store clerks stuck behind counters learn to leave their knees loose and keep their feet moving lest pinched blood vessels leave them in the fix you're in right now, Miss Rita. Don't have to peer up under your skirts to see you ain't been standing like an old soldier behind that faro layout. It's no big deal. We'll work these kinks out."

She said, "I'm starting to feel human again already. You're just an angel of mercy, Custis Long! It usually takes hours for that awful throbbing to go down. Do you have any other tricks to show me with those big amazing hands of yours?"

He calmly replied, "I reckon I might. But first you have

130

to tell me about them tears in your eyes, Miss Rita. Who are we talking about, a lover who used to rub your feet after work?"

She buried her face in her hands.

He insisted, "Miss Rita?"

She said, "I thought he was a lover. He turned out to be a pimp, before I killed him the summer before last in Virginia City."

Chapter 15

Longarm heard her out and made no value judgements as he resisted the temptation to hurry her tale. Every time they told it in the boom-and-bust towns of the west, they seemed to think such things had never happened to any other gals.

In this case, they'd called him Ace. He'd been a handsome dealer in cards and mining stock who'd stolen the heart of a preacher's daughter pledged to a man with 670 acres of bottomland, a reputation for paying his just debts and an inablity to carry a tune or dance worth mention. Her folk had warned they'd never have her back if she went out West with that tinhorn man. So after they'd been out West a spell she'd found that whilst Ace was a great kisser who gave swell foot massages, back rubs and other sorts of swell rubbings, they dined on pheasant under glass some nights and shared white bread and beans some others. Ace was better at joshing and drinking with the boys than he was at work, even had he thought a job wasn't beneath the dignity of a man of destiny. But he'd taught her to play cards when he wasn't . . . rubbing her, and they'd both been surprised to find she had a talent for the same as well as the looks to do better dealing faro, blackjack or whatever, as Rio Rita, along the upper Arkansas.

When Longarm gently asked how that made her Ace a pimp, she pouted, "What else would you call a man who lay about drunk whilst his woman brought in all the money, working like a slave?"

She dabbed at her eyes as Longarm went on massaging her feet. She looked away and softly confessed, "I was fool enough to put up with what he called a streak of hard luck far too long. You see, I really loved Ace, or I thought I did until the night there was a fight at the card house and they sent me home early to find Ace in bed with the married woman from next door! The place where I'd worked had issued me this Colt-Root .28 that was easy to hide under my skirts, and, oh, Custis, how could I have shot him like that when I loved him so?"

He gently pointed out, "If you hadn't loved him so you might not have shot him. What about that gal from next door?"

She shrugged and said, "They commended me for resisting the temptation, albeit in truth I felt nothing but cold contempt for the drab, and her husband left her as well. They gave me a suspended sentence under some provision they called the unwritten law."

Longarm said, "By definition the unwritten law can't be a law. It's a long-standing tradition. I reckon they saw that since you'd killed nobody but your husband, they could trust you not to do that again."

She grimaced and half-sobbed, "I never mean to wed a second time! A woman who can support herself as well as I can needs no man to mess up her quarters and demand to be fed at all hours like a baby robin in her nest!"

He nodded soberly and allowed he had serious reservations on the institution of marriage, having been to many a lawman's funeral and being not at all sure he wanted to live in an institution.

He said, "The theory sounds fine, but trying to make it work in practice can add up to a heavy row to hoe. Men and women both suffer the same delusion that they understand one another, or want the same things out of married life."

She drew her knees higher to pout, "Don't you think women are as wise as you owl birds perched above the pool hall?"

He laughed and conceded, "Maybe smarter, or more practical when it comes to country matters. That's not saying men and women *think* the same. Most women offer their fair white bodies hoping to find true love. Most men swear true love hoping to get at some fair white body."

She bitterly added, "Or as many fair white bodies as they can get at! You men will promise anything to have your wicked ways with us poor trusting fools!"

Longarm softly replied, "I try to confine my offers to flowers, books and candy, Miss Rita."

She wriggled her bare toes in his hands to ask, "What about foot rubs?"

He squeezed friendly and replied, "I offered to help out a pal with sore feet after she'd saved my life. If this constitutes an assault on your fair white body, so be it. Do you want me to stop?"

She hesitated, then nodded and decided he'd done about enough down yonder. So Longarm moved her feet around to leave her half-reclining as he rose to strap his gun back on.

"What are you doing? Are you *going* someplace, Custis? What about that nightcap? What about those scrambled eggs?"

He smiled down uncertainly to say, "I thought I just heard you say to stop, Miss Rita."

She rose to stand betwixt him and the way out, their bodies almost touching, as she husked, "I said you'd done

135

enough for my *feet*. Did I say the *rest* of me was satisfied?"

So he just kissed her and didn't ask what in thunder she'd been talking about. Men or women who demanded explanations for every whim of the moment got to study alone in the dark on how they might have messed things up. He just unbuckled his gun-rig, tossed it on that sofa and reeled her in for a howdy-kiss.

From the way Rio Rita kissed back, it was safe to assume she'd only soured on *formal* relationships with men, albeit later that night, sharing a cheroot and pillow talk after the protracted orgy following that first famished kiss, she confided she'd most often come home on her own after a weary evening on her aching feet, treating boisterous sporting men with the ill-disguised contempt she felt they deserved.

As they cuddled nude atop her crazy quilt with one of her restored feet roaming up and down the inside of his right shin, Rio Rita said he'd won her for the night before she'd saved his bacon at the Silver Dollar. She said, "I could see you didn't remember me from Virginia City. I was dealing blackjack, and you were after somebody else. You went through the motions of betting as you asked some polite questions, and then you thanked me sweetly, left a good tip, and drifted off to some other layout. They told me, after, you'd been the famous Longarm, feared by men and a terror with the ladies. I said at the time a man like you didn't terrify *this* lady, and, as I just found out, I knew what I was talking about. You sure know what you're doing with those clever hands!"

She reached down to fondle his recovering virile member as she said she hadn't meant to leave that part of him out, and then she asked how long he'd be in town.

Most women did, Lord love 'em.

He told her, "Can't say. At least until the county clears me on that shooting, and I manage to convince 'em they want the body to have and to hold. I didn't say anything about the bounty money posted on the late Mel Stuart, as Fuzzy Sinclair, because I didn't want Frank or Pappy wiring for it before I could have a friendly sit down with your sheriff or your Marshal Duggan. I don't much care who claims the remains as long as *I* don't have to pay for his funeral."

He thought, snuffed out the smoke they'd been sharing and decided, "Forty-eight to seventy-two hours to settle the matter of that shoot-out, earlier this evening. By then, I may or may not know whether the man I came for is still in town, if he was ever here. I hate it when they do that, but riders of the owlhoot trail are forever telling a pal they're headed one way when they mean to go somewhere else."

Summer nights got right cool a mile higher than Denver, so when Rio Rita got up to fix him that nightcap, she made it a hot toddy, heating the mix as she scrambled eggs with red peppers and onions before she got him to tell her all about Crimp Gooding and that remaining former pal who was after him. He didn't mind bringing her up-to-date as they picnicked atop her crazy quilt, her in a chemise and him in just his shirt against the chill of the mountain night. He figured a gal who dealt faro in the biggest saloon in town would have dealt a hand or two to most every sporting life in Leadville by then. But she just couldn't recall anybody bucking the tiger who answered to Crimp Gooding's description. She said she'd learned to avoid men with eyebrows meeting in the middle since she'd left home with one. Longarm agreed she'd have likely remembered Crimp Gooding from up close.

Freshening his mug from the tray she'd brought to bed, Rio Rita sounded resigned enough as she mused, "Then you'll be going on, or back to Pueblo, if you don't cut Mr. Gooding's trail in Leadville in the next day or so?"

He said that was about the size of it and added, "Can't

137

say, yet, whether they'll want me to return to Pueblo or hop the LC&SRR for the way shorter run down to Denver. Like I told you, my hunt for Crimp Gooding was an excuse to have me out of town while my own pals tried to cut that other killer's trail."

Rio Rita washed down some peppered eggs and onion before she made a face and flatly stated, "A six-foot-six woman with any color hair would surely stand out in a mostly male population of hard rock miners and mill hands. I don't see how she could be here in Leadville, Custis."

Longarm said, "Neither do I. She'd have no call to head up this way unless somebody around the Denver federal building talks to tall strangers. She's after *me*, not Crimp Gooding, or his late pal, Fuzzy Sinclair, and nobody was supposed to tell her *I* was headed up this way."

By the time they'd finished the warm food and drink, they were warm enough to toss her chemise and his shirt aside to give one another a brisk mutual rubdown with their bare bellies. Rio Rita complimented Longarm on his firm but gentle lovemaking, confiding she'd been just a little afraid he might live up to his reputation as a sex maniac.

He didn't tell her he liked to make love to any woman as she seemed to want the job done. None of them wanted to know. They all liked to feel it was their own grand notion to screw him as best they knew how.

He'd already noticed Rio Rita liked to start with a slow canter through the park, working up to a cross-country fox hunt at full gallop to jump a heap of fences toward the end of the chase. She was inclined to say silly things about healthy lust, and whilst Longarm hesitated to say anything mushy a gal might try to hold him to, he knew better than to talk dirty, fucking such a romantic-natured little thing.

Starting work at the Silver Dollar late in the day, Rio

Rita got to sleep late in the morning, and, by morning, they both needed some sleep.

Over the swell late breakfast Rio Rita rustled up for him, she tried to get Longarm to promise he'd pick her up that evening at the Silver Dollar. He warned he was a man of his word and couldn't make promises he wasn't sure he'd be able to keep.

When she watered up a mite, he soothingly explained, "Midnight is a long ways off, and we've both got chores to tend before we meet again, if we're fated to meet again. I got to tidy up that shooting with the local powers that be. It's their call how long that might take. After that, it's up to my home office to say whether I'm supposed to keep looking for Crimp Gooding here in Leadville or head somewhere else on the double. My boss, Marshal Vail, is a caution when it comes to tracking suspects on paper. I wired last night I'd be staying at the Chrysolite Hotel. Before I met up with you, that is to say. So for all I know, I have travel orders waiting at my hotel already, and farther along, as the old church song goes, we'll know more about it."

She pouted, "Do you expect me to just wait idly by with folded hands while you make up your mind whether you ever want to fuck me again?"

He smiled thinly and replied, "I just said it ain't up to me, and I never asked you to fold your hands when they could be dealing faro for fun and profit."

She said, "Others I could mention have often asked to walk me home after work, Custis. How dumb would I look if I said I alread had an understanding with someone, and my someone never showed up?"

He rose from her kitchen table to finish dressing as he agreed she'd sure look dumb and added, "We both got to do what we both got to do, Miss Rita. I'll try to be there before midnight. If I get there after midnight, and you've left with somebody else, I promise I won't get sore."

She quietly replied, "I know. That's what I was afraid of. But you're right, Custis. We're both gamblers, in our own ways, and we both have to play the cards we're dealt. I was just being a silly."

He assured her he hadn't thought she was being silly. White lies didn't count. They kissed more than once betwixt the time he was fully dressed and armed for action again and the time she let him out the door.

He ambled back to the business district and asked at the hotel desk if they had any telegraph wires in his pigeon hole. The skinny bald desk clerk said they had no wires from Denver, but handed over a notice from the Lake County Coroner's Office.

Longarm opened the envelope to see they were holding the inquest at the county courthouse at two that afternoon. They wanted him to be there. They didn't say what would happen if he failed to show. They didn't have to. There were only two railroad lines and a handful of mountain trails out of the valley.

He saw he had time to kill and moseyed over to the Western Union to wire another progress report. Passing a corner newsstand, he paused to stock up on smokes and saw the afternoon edition of the *Herald Democrat* was out, with his name on the front page.

In banner headlines.

He paid for the paper along with his cheroots and tucked it under his arm to carry it back to the hotel and read in private. It was bad enough the whole damned world would know he was in Leadville now. He had no call to frighten horses in the street when he really let loose with his feelings that afternoon!

Chapter 16

As he spread the local paper across his made-up bedstead in his hired room, Longarm saw things could have been worse. The rewrite editor for the *Herald Democrat* didn't seem to think he was Mark Twain. So unlike many a small town newspaper's account of a local shooting, the front page story got the facts about right and hadn't said the famous Longarm was checked into the Chrysolite Hotel.

After that, anybody gunning for Crimp Gooding would soon know his pal, Mel Stuart, aka Fuzzy Sinclair, had run off to Leadville in hopes of joining up with Gooding there. As if that hadn't been bad enough, Longarm now knew Increase Younger would now know where to look for him instead of down in Denver.

Calming himself down with a whole cheroot, Longarm lit another and went out again to send that wire to Billy Vail, tossing in the newspaper giveaway. He felt sure he'd soon receive orders to pack the snipe hunt in and head on back to Denver to hole up yonder whilst his pals watched out for that literally big sister of the late Cotton Younger.

Having the time to kill, Longarm drifted slowly up Harrison Avenue toward the courthouse where they'd be holding that inquest. At that hour, most everyone who had a job in Leadville would be working at it. But there were a heap of lost souls on the streets of Leadville at all hours who didn't care to work or just couldn't find a job.

Tales of towns shipping bullion by the ton always attracted more working stiffs than the biggest boom could hire, along with mayhaps as many hoping to get rich quick without having to work for it. The results, around Leadville, made it impossible for any obvious outsider to survive, and downright dangerous for an obviously *white* man. Down-on-their-luck drifters soon learned it was futile to bust a window in Leadville in hopes of a warm meal and a place to lay one's head in the local jail. The town law simply beat the liver and lights out of bums and ordered them out of town on pain of death. Jail cells in Leadville were reserved for *sincere* criminals. You had to kill somebody all the way or mayhaps rob a bank to get locked up in Leadville.

Despite their desperation, nobody had, as yet, robbed Silver Dollar Tabor's imposing two-story brick bank, distinguished, of course, by the huge disc of tinfoil-covered pine meant to resemble a silver dollar, erected atop the roof.

They said the mayor now owned sawmills supplying the building boom, the waterworks that served the mushrooming town, and insurance companies to underwrite the same, along with many an as-yet-unsold building lot, and, of course, countless mines he controlled outright or held shares in for miles around.

So far he'd backed one serious mistake, a horse-drawn streetcar company that hadn't worked when no horses could be found to pull street cars up steep grades that high above sea level.

The thin air didn't do wonders for malnourished drunks, and it was whispered innumerable bodies had been secretly cremated in one of the monsterous smelters close to town by orders of the chamber of commerce run by, who else, Silver Dollar Tabor.

Still having a few minutes to kill, Longarm stopped on the corner near the courthouse to watch the commotion occasioned by the skirl of bagpipes. With most of the working men busy and most of their wives at home, housekeeping or, rather, guarding the premises against roving bands of lumber thieves, there seemed to be mostly riffraff and kids lined up to admire the Tabor Highland Guards, all sixty-odd of them, resplendent in bearskin hats, Royal Stuart tartan and white goat-hair sporrans swishing across their kilts as they marched on to victory, or wherever in hell the flamboyant Horace Tabor thought he was headed at full gallop.

A society gal Longarm knew better had assured him the plain but well-liked Miss Augusta Tabor had raised their one son, Nat, to have her own common sense and decency. Hence whilst Silver Dollar pranced and flaunted his money and his mistresses, one reputed to be a circus performer who'd juggled with Indian clubs before she'd found a way to make a lot more lying down, Miss Augusta was becoming famous for her charity work amidst the poor and fallen all around them. So Longarm didn't doubt that when, not if Silver Dollar ever left his plain but sensible Augusta to live openly with Baby Doe, his Colorado empire would last no longer than a castle of cards.

As the bagpipes faded away into an uncertain future destination, Longarm went on to that coroner's inquest. One would never know it back East, from reading the colorful small town papers of the West, but when you shot a man dead, blew down your gun barrel and strode off with spurs all ajingle, you wound up with a corroded gun barrel, and they usually put out a wanted poster on your arrogant ass.

But it only took a few minutes in a side room of the

courthouse to convince the Lake County Coroner and his panel the shooting of the late Fuzzy Sinclair had been not only inevitable but justifiable. That deputy called Pappy was there to back Longarm's play, along with the morose City Marshal Duggan, who might have been desribed as a "shanty" by a Lace Curtain Irish Catholic or "Black Irish" by an Orange or Scotch Irishman. He really did have some notches carved into the grips of his Peacemaker. It was impossible to count them without appearing nosey.

Once the coroner had absolved Longarm of any criminal intent in gunning a known criminal in self-defense, Longarm took the local lawmen aside to deal with the financial considerations.

As he'd hoped, the minute they heard Fuzzy Sinclair had died with a price on his head, the two locals argued over who best deserved the notch for his own six-gun. In the end, it was decided that Pappy had assisted Longarm under the direct orders of Marshal Duggan. So they'd put in for the bounty fifty-fifty and naturally bury the son of a bitch for such a generous visiting lawman who'd done little more than pull the trigger.

Duggan had been the one who'd heard Sinclair was in town and sent Pappy to the Silver Dollar to arrest him, the three of them agreed.

So they shook on it and parted friendly.

Back at the Western Union, they told Longarm they'd recieved no reply to his earlier wire to Marshal Vail. That saved him asking at the front desk when he went back to his hotel for his saddle and bridle.

Suspecting old Billy Vail, speaking of Scotchmen, would hold off until he could reply by night-letter rates, sent after business hours at half price, Longarm figured he'd as soon cover a few more bets than hang around doing nothing until he knew whether he'd be hopping a night train or Rio Rita.

So he toted his heavily laden McClellan to the nearest livery and hired a barrel-chested Spanish saddle mule, not a pony, to carry a man as big as him at such high altitude.

Longarm was half broken-in to the thin air of Leadville, having spent so much time a mile above sea level around the state capital. Many a newcomer arriving from sea level wound up in that new Saint Vincent's General, or turned right around to go somewheres they could still breathe.

Longarm's reasons for riding a Spanish saddle mule that afternoon seemed simple enough. If Crimp Gooding was up this way at all, he had to be laying mighty low in town or working somewhere outside the main settlement. Aside from the many mines, stamping mills, smelters, produce or dairy farms and such, there were outlying hamlets such as California Gulch, Carbonate, Fryer's Luck, Mica, Strayhorse Gulch and such where a man could find food, drink, the more desperate sort of whores, or, of course, a game of chance.

Having heard of such actions out along the Chicken Bill Road towards the Chrysolite lode his hotel was named for, Longarm decided to ride that way first.

Chrysolite was a carbonate ore of lead and silver that eroded down to heavy blue-black sand early gold prospectors had found a bother until they'd found out what was gumming up their sluice runs. The first color found along California Gulch had been raw placer gold, glinting pretty in the high-country sunlight once you washed it free of that pesky black sand that refused to float on by like *sand* was *supposed* to.

An ambitious failed prospector named Horace Austin Tabor, or most likely his smarter wife, had been among the first to find out such shitty black sand assayed forty ounces of silver to the ton. Since somebody had to support them, old Augusta had done laundry and taken in boarders until she'd parlayed their cabin into a general store. Her feckless man, still panning gold unskillfully and making less at it than anyone panning within miles, would have grubstaked his pals on credit had not Miss Augusta insisted on IOUs against future strikes. By the time hungry prospectors had discovered the delights of blue-black chrysolite under overburdens of greenish white hard-as-hell porphyry or sheets of rusty iron ore contaminated with gold dust, the Tabors had moved their modest operations to nearby Slabtown, voted with others to rename it Leadville, and grown rich as all get-out without having to work half as hard.

It hardly seemed fair, but once you got rich, getting richer was duck-soup simple. "Tabor's Luck," as they called it, had included being suckered by a salted mine, telling his hands they might as well dig down a ways, and hitting chrysolite paying $100,000 a month ever since.

Chicken Bill Lovell, the knavish old rogue who'd sold the Tabors a salted mine worth millions, had sold almost as rich a claim for some drinking money, "outside the mineralized area," to a greenhorn now known as Mining Magnate George Fryer. Hence Chicken Bill Road in deference to such a slicker's grasp on geology.

A mile or so outside of town, just out of sight from the same, Longarm spied a buckboard stalled in the narrow wagon trace ahead. As he rode on, Longarm made out a trim figure in a sky blue dress perched on the spring seat, looking somehow tense, even at such a distance. As he rode closer, he saw a trio of four shabby men on foot apparently disputing the right of way. One had hold of the one horse's bridle. The other two were holding rifles across their chests at port arms. The last time Longarm had heard of such bullshit it had been out along Ten Mile Road.

To save a heap of needless bother, before riding on, Longarm got out his wallet, unpinned his federal badge from the same and stuck it to the lapel of his frock coat.

146

Then he drew his Winchester '73 from its saddle boot, levered a round of .44-40 in the chamber, and heeled his Spanish saddle mule forward.

To Longarm's chagrin, they stood their ground when they spied him coming to join the discussion. He'd expected them to light out. They were likely more desperate than some.

As he rode closer, he could see they were young, too. Teenaged trash whites with guns could act dumb as hell. Longarm recalled he'd been in his teens at a place called Shiloh when he'd killed his first human being, another teenager who hadn't known there were other ways to point a gun.

When he got close enough for them to make out his badge, one of them called out, "We ain't doing nothing wrong out here, lawman. We got us a permit from Mayor Tabor hisself to collect tolls on this turnpike."

The one holding the visibly upset woman's cart horse jovially chimed in, "You've doubtless seen our poor old uncle, Abe Lee, trying to lay the dust of Leadville with his water cart. We're amassing money to pave the streets and this here road by collecting tolls out this way."

Riding closer with his Winchester's muzzle held politely high and ready to throw down on anyone he had a mind to, Longarm gravely told them, "Of course I know your Uncle Abe. Hasn't everyone heard how Miss Augusta Tabor invented that tedious but easy chore for old Abe Lee after he went bust? She must have figured it was the least the town could do for the old-timer who'd made the first strike over in California Gulch. He sent me out this way with a message for you sons of . . . his favorite sister. He said he'd changed his mind about having you boys collect tolls for him. He said he owed it to his favorite sister to see you boys lived past this very day."

One of them shifted the Spencer .52 he was holding at port. Then he found himself staring straight up the steady barrel of a '73 Winchester .44-40 as Longarm whip-cracked, "Don't. I ain't fixing to say that again."

The one holding the bridle volunteered in a tone of forced amusement, "Maybe we'd better go back to town and talk to Uncle Abe, boys. No sense getting ourselves all sweaty over an honest misunderstanding, is there?"

When the others agreed, Longarm said that sounded jake with him as long as they passed betwixt him and the wagon instead of moving behind it, where somebody might think somebody else was about to fire from cover.

They followed his directions with almost indecent haste. Longarm sat his mount staring soberly after them until he saw they were out of easy rifle range. Then, doubting any of them would have the skills or the nerve to risk pegging a long rifle shot, Longarm turned to the gal frozen in place on the buckboard seat to tick his hat to her and say, "Your servant, ma'am. War's over with no casualties on either side. I'm Deputy U.S. Marshal Custis Long, and I'd be proud to escort you as far as that shanty town they say I'll find at the dead end of this road."

A familar voice replied, uncertainly, "Oh, Good Heavens, it's *you* again! But what did you mean about a dead end? Doesn't this wagon road lead over the Front Range to Denver?"

Smiling down at Miss Rowena Burnes of the tea-colored hair and a head for figures, Longarm politely but firmly informed her, "These wagon ruts hardly go any-wheres, 'cept past one of Mayor Tabor's numerous claims, Miss Rowena. Mayhaps you'd better tell me why in thunder you'd be headed for Denver by buckboard so late in the day."

Chapter 17

Her tale took little time to be told and held few surprises for a man who'd spent more time in boomtowns. By the time she'd filled him in on a boss who'd demanded bedroom privileges as well as bookkeeping for piss-poor pay, Longarm had dismounted to lead her horse around, upslope, and get her turned back towards town. She'd said she wanted to go to Colorado Springs, the Little London of Colorado where it was said even hoboes washed behind the ears before leaving the rail yards. The Chicken Bill wagon trace led no such place.

As he remounted his hired mule, she explained how she'd invested the last of her savings in the sway-backed nag and worn-out buckboard he'd found her and her modest baggage aboard.

He said, "Seeing it's getting late and I was likely on a fool's errand, and those young tramps could be skulking up the trail, I'll tell you what we'd better do, Miss Rowena. We'd better see if I can get you anything for that horse and cart when I return this mule where I hired it. If they won't give you enough for a narrow-gauge ticket, I reckon I lend you the fare to the Springs by way of Denver aboard the Leadville, Colorado and Southern.

What were you planning on doing in the Springs, if you don't mind my asking?"

She sobbed, "I mean to wire collect to see if the man I never should have spurned will still have me! I was a fool to think I was capable of making it on my own as a woman and now *you're* trying to do it, too!"

He clucked her horse and his mule to action before he mildly asked what he was supposed to be up to.

He found it awkward to ride beside her buckboard seat on such a narrow mountain trail. He felt more awkward when she sniffed and said, "Oh, come now, we both know what you're after! I've yet to have a man offer to pay my way in to a ballroom without having something else in mind!"

He dropped back and swung his left boot to the wagon bed to step aboard, drop to one knee with the reins in his hand and tether the mule to a cross brace before he moved forward to swing a long leg over and join her on the sprung seat, offering to drive if she'd care to listen.

She said she knew how to drive, dammit, and added, "Don't you dare put your arm up along the back of this seat, good sir!"

He leaned the other way, saying, "Perish the thought. I was about to observe you might not have given many men the chance to treat you with any consideration, Miss Rowena. But I see you know it all and I'll only ask how come, if you have a swain on tap who might send for you with a pure heart, how come you didn't wire him from Leadville and save yourself the cost of this hopeless transportation?"

She didn't answer for a time. When she did she explained, in a small embarrassed voice, "I didn't know they *had* a Western Union in Leadville! I never thought to *ask*! You see? I *do* need a man I can trust to tell me what to do!"

He gently pointed out, "Miss Rowena, what you're suggesting is a contradiction in terms. Trust a man who knows the ways of most men with maids dumb enough to trust them. Men a maid ought to trust can seldom be found, and that's the truth."

She shot an arch look at him as she asked, "Are you trying to convince me *you* can be trusted, Deputy Long?"

He chuckled and confessed, "Of course not. I think you're purdy. But since we've established that you don't trust me or most other men, I don't see what you're worried about. I ain't offering you common decency with strings attached. I told you I expected an IOU for any hard cash I expended on your rescue from that vile wine theater boss. So pay attention. Are you paying attention, Miss Rowena?"

When she half sobbed that she seemed to have no choice, he said, "Bueno. I can't leave Leadville before I have wired permission from my own boss. So I don't see how we'd be able to board the night train out just after sundown. But I still have a reasonably civilized room at a reputable hotel, so . . ."

"Here it comes!" Rowena declared to the road ahead.

He said, "You ain't paying attention. I won't be staying there at the Chrysolite tonight. You'll be, alone, if you can contain your disappointment. The hire of the room's paid up and there's no sense either of us sleeping on an unpaved street. When we get into town, I'd best take the reins so's I can drop you off at my hotel and let you wait in the lobby whilst I carry this wagon and both critters to that livery and see what I can get for you. Before you ask how you'll know I ain't cheated you, what did you pay and I'll see if I can get you fifty cents on the dollar."

She said she'd laid out twenty-five dollars, or nigh a month's wages for unskilled labor, and allowed twelve dollars and fifty cents didn't sound fair.

He said he'd try to get 'em up to fifteen, explaining, "No horse trader is fixing to give you more than half of

151

what he thinks he can sell his investment for. You paid too much to begin with, no offense."

She handed him the reins to leave both hands free to cover her weepy eyes. Longarm grimaced and bit back his obvious observation about independent women.

As Longarm and Rowena Burnes were making their way back to Leadville, another woman who thought she was independent was reading a Pueblo paper at her kitchen table, grinning wolfishly as she pictured the Fargo Kid up in Denver spying the same headlines.

The story of the shooting of Fuzzy Sinclair, aka the same Mel Stuart Pueblo readers might recall from the recent trial of the Fargo Kid, had gained some flourishes as other papers picked up the original article in the *Herald Democrat*. But all Increase Younger cared about was that she was one down with two to go, courtesy of the very man she'd sent the Fargo Kid after, and now the Fargo Kid would know his target was in Leadville, a short narrow-gauge hop from Denver!

She heard the creak of a gate and glanced out the window to see Deputy Roy Manx crossing her hired back yard with a box of chocolates, the pestiferous son of a bitch!

She'd only cleaned out that secret room in the cellar and still had to take down that false wall and reerect it, shelves and all, against the real rear far end, down yonder. What on earth was the married simp doing there at that hour?

She asked him as he came in to give her the chocolates and a French kiss, standing tiptoe as he did so. She kissed him back as dirty and ground her pubic bone against his gut before he managed to tell her, "I just couldn't hold out 'til noon tomorrow, huggy bunny! But you may be right. We may not have much time. So can we get right to it?"

She pretended to give a shit as she led him into her bedroom sort of growling, the way she knew he found exciting. Like many a married up simp, he didn't seem to understand how a woman who didn't really give a shit could give a better ride, the way a detached barber was able to give a better haircut than some nervous beginner.

She shucked her kimono and flopped languidly across her covers as she asked in a conversational tone how he managed to service her most every noon, his wife most every night, and still stop by for a quickie on his way home.

As he fumbled out of his own duds, Roy Manx confessed, "I ain't been getting any at home, lately. At breakfast this very morning she accused me right out of seeing someone like you on the side!"

Increase rolled on her broad back to spread her massive thighs as she demanded, "How do you think she got that idea? Haven't you been doing her right at home the way I suggested, you brute?"

Manx got in bed with her and snuggled close to strum her old banjo as he replied, "I tried to do her better, French, the way you like it! But she got all hystericated and demanded to know who taught me such crimes against nature!"

Increase purred, "Get down there and use that sweet tongue with criminal intent while we study on this, Roy! Arc you sure you haven't bragged to any of your pals about . . . the way I blow the French horn for you?"

He rolled between her upraised knees and stooped to cunt-lick as he lied, "Of course not! What kind of a cuss would tattle on a loving little thing who liked to blow him?"

Then he began to blow her as she mused aloud, "Nine out of ten men, I suppose. We're going to have to get some other secrets straight, darling, now that even your wife seems to know about us. I told you I'd been in prison and my first name really is Creasy, for Increase. But I fear I fibbed when I told you my last name was James. I'm not a Miss Increase James trying to start all over out this way. I fear I'm really Increase Younger, the sister of the late notorious Cotton Younger, you may well have heard about."

Roy Manx raised his head from her lap to gasp, "Jesus full of jumping beans! We've got an all-points out on you at the office! The federal marshal in Denver wired you were fixing to murder one of his own deputies!"

She draped a calf over his bare behind as she sighed and said, "I know. That's why I thought I'd better own up to my true name, darling. My brother, Cotton Younger, was killed by the famous Longarm whilst I was in prison. Somebody seemed to think I'd be stupid enough to go after Longarm when I got out, even though I'm only a girl, and, as I told you, anxious to start over after all those years lost to an earlier mistake! But do I look like I'm stalking Deputy U.S. Marshal Long up Leadville way, where the papers say he just shot somebody else?"

Roy Manx sat up and ran his fingers through his thinning hair as he marveled, "Jesus H. Christ, I've been shacked up with a murder suspect and if this gets out, they'll have my badge if my wife don't kill me first! You should have told me sooner, girl! What in thunder am I to do about this?"

She said, "Well, fucking me some more might be a nice start. After that you can turn me in for all I care. You'll find that when push comes to shove in front of any judge, I haven't done anything they can put either one of us in jail for, aside from a few teeny-weeny violations of the state sodomy statutes, that is."

He smiled uncertainly but with dawning hope as he decided, "That's right! You haven't made one hostile move against any lawman at all unless you count those fingernail marks I had a time explaining at home! I ain't about to admit cunt-licking or corn-holing in open court, but do they accuse me of aiding and abetting I stand ready to prove, you can ask my friends, if you ain't been here in Peublo all this time and . . . Say, come to study on it, you were here in Pueblo when that Longarm gent passed through, searching high and low for Crimp Gooding, and you never made one hostile move against the man!"

"You said he was in town, if you care to remember," she chimed in, adding, "You know I like to hear about your day at the office, you big lug."

Manx brightened and said, "That's true! I did mention the Denver lawman we sent on his way up the river after Gooding. And I told you about Gooding's gal, Trixie Davis, headed east the other way!"

She held out her arms in welcome as she asked in a confused tone why she should be interested in anyone named Gooding or Davis. As he fell forward to be hugged while he steered his raging erection into her gaping love maw, he asked himself the same question. They'd said she might be after that federal man from Denver. Nothing had been suggested about her being tied in with the Fargo Kid's case.

As she pursed her love-lips tight around his throbbing shaft, the literal monster he was penetrating *knew* there wasn't one thing to connect her with the Fargo Kid and his own chosen targets, whether he lived through his encounter with Longarm or not. What had he expected after she'd busted him out of jail a hop, skip and a jump from the gallows, an egg in his beer?

As she moved her massive hips to play another sucker on her line, she reflected petulantly that she'd sent the Fargo Kid on his way as thoroughly satisfied and walking funny. What was he going to do after he killed Longarm for her? Sue her for breach of murder contract? With any luck, he'd still be wondering whether Crimp and Trixie were dead or alive when they met up Cheyenne way as agreed. If she found *him* still alive, she'd remedy that fast and collect the price on the head of a wanted killer!

"What are you laughing about, huggy bunny?" Roy Manx asked without missing a stroke.

She crooned, "I'm just giggling because you tickle a girl so fine with that big old love tool, darling! I swear if you were hung any bigger, I'd never be able to take you on like this! I'd be lying if I said I was a blushing cherry, Roy. But you are really something else, next to most men I've known!"

This was bullshit, of course, but as she'd known he would, Roy Manx ate it up. He'd often wondered how he measured up to other men, but when he'd asked his wife, she'd wept and swore and torn her hair at the intimation she was in any position to *know*!"

More than one hooker had told him he was hung good and knew how to use what he had better than most men. But you had to take the praise of a *hooker* with a pinch of salt.

Hookers, Roy Manx knew as he let himself go with Creasy, pretended to like everybody they were paid to screw. But this good old gal had never asked for a thing from him but a thorough reaming from a man whose wife just didn't seem to appreciate his screwing and refused to even consider any position but old-fashioned, with her infernal nightgown on!

He kissed his partner in adultery warmly as he tried to hit bottom the way she liked it, sure that she was telling him the truth about the way she felt about his inspired virility. For why would this one lie if she didn't really *like* him?

Chapter 18

Meanwhile, up in Leadville, Longarm had left Rowena Burnes on the buckboard and gone into his hotel to bet the desk clerk a dollar they couldn't do things his way.

Once he'd lost, he deposited Rowena and his saddle in the lobby to argue with them later and drove the buckboard and bareback Spanish saddle mule back to the livery so's he'd only have to come back with the bridle. They were willing to take the sway-backed nag and broken-down wagon off his hands, but they told him anyone who'd paid twenty-five whole dollars for the whole she bang had been suckered.

Longarm reflected on how lucky the spunky young gal had been that Chicken Bill Road hadn't led anywhere, with night coming on, and said he'd take the ten for the horse and the five for the wagon. *He'd have never paid that much*, but dog meat and firewood were scarce in a boom town.

He toted his own army bridle back to the Chrysolite Hotel to find Rowena in an agiated snit. She looked relieved to see him and stood up betwixt his saddle and her carpetbag on the floor to either side to confess she's started to suspect he'd ditched her.

He said, "I always ditch gals in my own hotel, Miss Rowena, but if you'd be good enough to pick up your own baggage, I'll wrangle that saddle and we can talk about it upstairs."

It wouldn't have been polite to ask how often she'd been ditched. It sure beat all how many difficult women he'd been meeting up with of late. The high altitude likely had something to do with it.

She followed him and his McClellan, protesting all the way she'd never been up to any man's hotel room before. But he assured her there was always a first time and added this was an unusual experience for him as well.

Unlocking the door with his free hand, Longarm waved her and her carpetbag in, followed to drape the saddle over the foot of the bed but left the hall door open as he reached in his pants for a twenty-dollar gold piece.

Handing it over, he said he was sorry, but that was all he'd been able to get for her horse and cart. As she stared down dubiously, he confessed, "All right, I put five away as my commission."

She quicky replied it wasn't that she didn't trust him.

He nodded and said, "I know. You're trying to figure how you're to survive until that swain you never should have said no to wires you some more."

She sighed and said, "You mean *if*. I said some cruel things when I turned him down, and he's had time to find another."

Longarm suggested, "Maybe you'd better see if you can find another *job* when we get into Denver. There must be more than one position open for a bookkeeping gal in a city that size, and, no offense, I'm sure you're better off supporting your ownself than relying on a man you never wanted in the first place. A lot of married women have assured me of that."

She pointed out they were a long ways from Denver as she glanced tensely at the open door to the hall.

He said, "You got all night, at least, to study on it. We might or might not be on our way about this time tomorrow, or even earlier, if there's a night letter allowing me to call off my snipe hunt, come the cold gray dawn. We might have time for a good night's sleep, a hearty breakfast, and still catch the *noonday* narrow gauge back to Denver if my boss has a lick of sense."

She gulped and conceded, "Well, if we were to spread that bedroll from your saddle on the rug, and you promised to behave . . ."

"I don't make foolish promises," he cut in, adding, "I won't be here to tempt you, Miss Rowena. If you want anything from downstairs whilst I'm out, they'll put it on my bill and we can settle up later. When you want to turn in for the night, just slide that barrel bolt on yon hall door shut and no matter what my home office says, I'll be back before nine in the morning."

"Where do *you* mean to sleep, then?" she asked in a confused tone.

He said, "I'll think of something. Don't worry about me. Worry about *you*, and whether keeping books or a loveless marriage might hurt the most. You'll be arriving in Denver with hotel and eating money to last you over a week, and if you can't find a job in a week in a city that size, you sure ain't much of a bookkeeper, no offense."

He left her to her own devices and gently shut the hall door as he left. The sun set early in a mountain valley but left the clear sky above flamingo-belly pink for quite a spell in summertime. So they hadn't lit the street lamps as he moseyed over to State Street through the tricky light of gloaming.

Thus he wasn't certain of what he was seeing as a husky gent with ivory gun grips aglow in the waning light brushed by the other way through the evening rush. So Longarm paused as if to light a smoke before he turned to follow what might or might not answer to the description of the one and original Crimp Gooding!

The cuss was crossing the street at an angle, now, and Longarm had to pause to let a beer dray pulled by six mules rumble past. Once it had, he couldn't make out the figure he'd been following in the uncertainly lit confusion ahead.

"Lost him, you asshole!" Longarm grumbled as he continued the same way a while, cussed himself again and headed on over to State Street.

For if that *had* been Crimp Gooding and he *was* out after dark for action, such action as a stranger might find in Leadville after dark would be yonder.

The night was still young, so Longarm drifted into one wine theater after another, ordering a beer instead of wine, albeit at the *price* of wine, to nurse it standing at the bar as he scanned the crowd seated at tables facing the more or less identical stages at one end or the other.

The show at the Comique was shocking until you figured out that more than pleasantly plump lady was only wearing a flesh-colored union suit under that hula skirt and fake flower necklace.

But nobody in the crowd looked like Crimp Gooding at any of the wine theaters, so he wound up hunting for his material witness at Madame Vestal's Dance Hall, as it was called.

Singling out one man or a giraffe of modest size in *that* swirling crowd made a hard row to hoe. But on reflection, he saw there was a sort of counterclockwise swirl to the crowd of dancing couples. So Longarm once more positioned himself with his back to the bar and a right expensive dinky stein of beer in his left hand, figuring that sooner or later most every couple would come swirling by.

The odds against Crimp Gooding being out yonder on that floor to begin with were modest. But everybody, including Longarm, had to be somewhere, sometime. So what the hell.

He started to sip some more suds, reflected on how many sips he'd already put away within such a short interval and muttered, "Now you've had too much to drink, and they say he packs a Remington-Beals worn low and tied down!"

But the beer he'd already put away had him feeling mellow enough as he saw Gooding didn't know what he looked like. Gooding thought he was only running from the Fargo Kid. So how tough would it be to get the drop on him?

"Steady on, old hoss," he warned himself aloud, "Let's not talk about getting the drop on a cuss Billy Vail only wants us to bring in as a *witness*, if that!"

His mutterings gave the dance hall gal who'd been sizing him up a chance to sidle closer and ask, "You talking to me, handsome?"

He stared down a tad owlishly at the gal who looked about sixteen until you stared into her age-old eyes of weary cold-dawn gray. Her bodice was cut low to declare her tits were still firm and her Rainy Suzie skirts showed a hint of stocking above her high-button shoes.

He knew the barkeep was watching, and he knew what barkeeps in such places thought of beer nursers. So, not wanting to lose his vantage point, he smiled down at the pretty little drab to reply, "I was just waxing philosophic, ma'am. Has it ever occured to you that time is nature's way of preventing everything from happening all at once?"

She didn't laugh. But she smiled when he added, "What are you drinking this evening, pretty lady?"

She confided they called her Frenchy and allowed she'd like a flute of champagne.

He told the barkeep hovering near to serve the poor thirsty lady some of their fine vintage lemon soda in a wine flute, and the three of them laughed like fellow conspirators.

As Frenchy accepted her fake champagne, she said she'd noticed her gallant drinking partner seemed mighty intent on the dancers passing by. She asked, "Have you taken a fancy to one of our other dancing partners, or are you one of those bashful boys who never learned the waltz or two-step?"

He smiled thinly and said, "I've been wondering what on earth some of those dancers think they're up to. Some are waltzing, some are as you just suggested, two-stepping, whilst others seem to be trying to roller skate without the skates. But ain't that a Polka they're playing, Miss Frenchy?"

She laughed and said, "I can polka, if you'd care to ask me. You'd be surprised at some of the things I can do, if a man I like cares to *ask* me."

He sighed and said, "Just my luck, I'm on duty and can't ask, Miss Frenchy. I ain't watching the swirling skirts out on the floor. I am looking for a big heavyset cuss with eyebrows as meet in the middle and a Remington-Beals worn tied-down."

The barkeep who'd been listening in said, "Madame Vestal runs this place respectable, and we frown on troublemakers, Mister!"

Longarm said, "I ain't trouble. I'm the law. The man I'm looking for, mild, is only wanted for questioning."

Frenchy lit out like a scalded cat. The barkeep couldn't, so he told Longarm they had a deal with Marshal Duggan and a heap of folk were going to be pissed as hell if he shot anybody on the premises.

Longarm had just assured the worried barkeep he doubted his man was on said premises when there the jasper was, roller skating past with a bleached blond who could have lost thirty pounds without it hurting her looks at all. So Longarm put down his nigh-full stein and lit out after them, across the floor without a partner as he called out, "Rein her in, Gooding! I'm the law, and we got to talk!"

Then a mining man with a skinny brunette dancing partner and a couple of drinks too many under his belt crashed into Longarm and called him a cocksucker.

Longarm grabbed the skinny brunette to keep her from crashing headfirst to the waxed floor as he told the mining man he was sorry.

The mining man, who looked to be somewhat younger and almost as big as Longarm bellowed, "Unhand that poor damsel, you mother-fucking, baby-raping cocksucking son of a bitch!"

So Longarm set the gal steady on her own two feet and decked the asshole with one sucker punch, and everyone else got the hell out of Longarm's way as he forged on across the floor after Crimp Gooding and that fat gal.

But when he caught up with the fat bleached blond by a side exit, he found her confused and alone. He asked which way Crimp had gone, and she pointed at the doorway, volunteering, "He went out to the alley if that was his name! I swear I never saw him before if he's in trouble with the law!"

Longarm tore outside without answering, crabbing to one side lest the light from inside outline him as he peered up and down the dark alley in vain for any sign of that bulky but elusive cuss.

He jogged out to the street and circled the block, peering into window after window as hope faded.

Stopping in front of a cigar store to catch his breath and light a cheroot, Longarm confided to the cigar store's wooden Indian, "We've fucked it up entire, Chief. Now he knows I'm looking for him and he knows what I look like. What would *you* do in a situation such as this one?"

The cigar store Indian never answered. But Longarm shook out his match and said, "You're right. By now he's

163

gone to ground for the night, likely making plans to leave town under cover of darkness. We weren't supposed to let him do that, but we did, and it's a good thing he ain't a serious want."

He snorted smoke out both nostrils like a pissed off bull, told the wooden Indian it had been nice talking to him, and resumed his hunt for Crimp Gooding, knowing full well the slicker would be under a wet rock and fixing to stay there a spell.

Idly wondering who or what Gooding had taken him for, Longarm hit a few more hot spots before. Seeing it was getting late, he ambled on to the Silver Dollar, muttering, "All right, Crimp, if you don't want me guarding your ass from that Fargo Kid, I may as well find out if Rio Rita still likes me!"

It was hard to tell as he joined the others around the chestnut-haired faro dealer's table. He couldn't seem to catch her copper-colored eye as she had the late night sports really bucking her tiger for serious stakes.

Some called it bucking the tiger when you played against the faro shoe because for a long time in the beginning faro dealers had favored Tiger brand card decks with orange and black Bengal tigers printed on their backs. But after a while, smart money boys noticed how often the stripes on those tigers didn't quite match up and word got around, fast, about certain faro dealers filling in betwixt the printed stripes with India ink to hint at how the face sides might read. So Faro dealers who'd survived the wave of outrage across the land used other brands of late, albeit you were still said to buck the tiger when you played such a sucker's game.

A million years later, as all things must, the action at Rio Rita's table died down, and Longarm was able to take advantage of a lull to howdy her and say he'd wait by the bar until she got off.

"Aren't you taking a lot for granted, Custis?" she replied in a tone he couldn't decide on.

He didn't bite. He nodded knowingly and turned away as, behind him, Rio Rita hesitated, then called after him, "Wait, Custis. I only meant we have to get a few things straight between us, see?"

He'd seen. Rio Rita wasn't the first gal who'd ever warned him not to take her for granted, and he knew what she wanted to get straight. But *he'd* warned *her* how things had to be, and things weren't supposed to get that tedious until they'd spent more than one fucking night at fucking, for Pete's sake!

Saving himself the needless expense of another nursed beer, Longarm kept going and didn't look back until he'd parted the bat-wing doors to the street and quit whilst he was ahead. Having seen how it could be done on the streets of Leadville, he cut across against the traffic lest she tear ass out of the Silver Dollar after him. He'd been around *that* block, too, and sure felt like a fool after he'd given a gal a *second* chance to bitch him after she'd bitched him *once*.

He treated himself to a late snack at an all-night chili parlor and went on back to his hotel, where he asked the night clerk to hire him a room for the night. The older man behind the desk looked confused and asked if there was something wrong with the room he alread had, upstairs.

Longarm said, "There is. There's somebody else sleeping in that room. Don't get your bowels in an uproar. I already worked that part out with the desk clerk you relieved this evening."

"You gave your own room to someone else?" the night man asked.

To which Longarm could only reply, "I had other plans for the night. Or I thought I did. But what the hell, you can't win 'em all!"

Chapter 19

The next morning Longarm woke up early with a hard-on, drained his bladder, tidied up as best he could with all his shit locked away with Rowena Burnes, and went to the Western Union to see if there was a night letter from his home office.

There was. Billy Vail had agreed that since nothing resembling a six-foot-six Increase Younger had been seen in or about Denver, she'd likely sent that death threat in the first flush of getting out of prison, taken time to study on it, and decided not to risk her newfound freedom after all.

When Longarm got to the part about old desertion charges against Crimp Gooding hardly being worth the candle, Longarm forgot about wiring Vail he'd spotted the want and lost him the night before. It made no sense to *him* to spend any more time at that altitude and those prices just to bring back a want they were almost certain to let go. President Hayes had even forgiven the former Confederate states for the war.

He went back to the hotel to rouse Rowena from her beauty sleep. He found her up and dressed when he arrived. He didn't ask her if she'd taken a piss. He said, "It looks like we'll be catching that noon train down to Denver after all. Let's go have breakfast whilst I bring you up to date, Miss Rowena."

She allowed she was hungry but said something dumb about paying her own fair share. He waited until they were seated across from each other in the dining room of the more imposing Tabor Hotel before he asked her not to embarrass him in public by having others take him for a kept man or worse."

She laughed at the picture but said, "Honestly Custis, you've done enough for me already, and I don't know how I'll ever be able to repay you!"

Then she blushed and flustered, "I'm not that kind of a girl!"

He reached across the tablecloth to pat her wrist as he assured her he knew full well what sort of girl she was. It wouldn't have been polite to go into further detail.

Checking the time, he saw they had time for a serious late breakfast or early noon dinner. She said she could go for waffles with bacon if he'd let her pay for 'em. He ordered that for her and told the waiter he'd have his fried eggs over a T-bone and added they both wanted a heap of coffee to see them through a tedious train ride.

As their waiter left, Rowena smiled in mock severity to demand, "A T-bone steak for *breakfast*, Custis? *You* need someone to look after *you* as well!"

He said, "Already got someone to watch over me. I see him in the looking glass most every time I shave. Once we get to Denver you'll be free pay your own way in public. Whilst you're with me, I'm paying and let's hear no more about it, hear?"

"Yes, daddy," she meekly replied in a little girl voice.

As they waited on their late breakfast, Longarm explained about the night letter from his home office freeing them to hop that LC&SRR narrow gauge at the north terminal at Seventh Street betwixt Hemlock and Hazel.

He explained, "Shay locomotive pushes and pulls on alternate switchbacks climbing over the Front Range from Denver. Our ride *out* will be backing *in* to drop off passengers and freight from the mile-high lowlands around noon. Won't be headed back right off. But we'd best get there early in any case. They'll be leaving as soon as they load up for the return trip, and you just never know who or what might want to go down to Denver. The heavy ingots cast by the smelters all about travel separate, under armed guard."

She asked in a worried tone whether the LC&SRR got held up often.

He shook his head and said, "That's how come they send the silver bullion and lead pigs under armed guard. In the unlikely event some desperados *did* stop a narrow-gauge train in such steep surroundings, where would they *ride* with loot that heavy? Twenty dollars worth of silver adds up to more than a pound of dead weight, Miss Rowena. Any train robbers out for bullion would stop a *gold* shipment from, say, Central City, Gregory Gulch, Idaho Springs or such. Leadville is sort of tame for a mining town."

She repressed a shudder as she tried to picture a wilder scene than the one he was rescuing her from. Before she could get too mushy, the waiter brought their grub and they dug in for a spell to put away the same.

Rowena declared he couldn't be serious when he opted for dessert with more coffee. He warned her, "It's almost dinner time; there won't be any dining car or even a candy butcher on the narrow gauge and it's fixing to take us most of the afternoon to cover more than a hundred mighty twisty miles. They got drinking water and . . . facilities aboard the LC&SRR, but nothing fancier, and they don't stop halfway for grub like that longer line up the valley from Pueblo did the other day."

So she said in that case, she'd have some ice cream,

and he told the waiter he'd have *his* ice cream with a slice of mince pie.

As they dawdled, killing time with nothing better to do before they had to get on over to the terminal, the gal with a natural head for details extracted more about his curious snipe hunt out of him. She was one of those civilians who'd been led to believe nobody ever got away from the law.

He explained how his field mission had just been a make-work ploy to excuse his being away from his usual haunts whilst his pals staked 'em out to see if they could trap that big old crazy lady.

He said, "Some smaller figure in *pants* got my boss all excited until they decided it was likely some fool writer out to pester me for the story of my life. I warned Ned Buntline I'd take him to court if he ever did a job on me like he did on poor James Butler Hickok. Buffalo Bill Cody's made out all right as one of Buntline's dime magazine characters. But he got Hickok *killed* when Cockeyed Jack McCall read all that puffery and decided *he* wanted to be a character, too."

She asked if he was saying Buffalo Bill and Wild Bill Hickok were big phonies. He shook his head and assured her, "Bill Cody really rid for the pony express as a lad, shot all that buffalo meat to feed the track crews of the Missouri Pacific, not the Union Pacific as some say, and really did shoot a Cheyenne called Yellow Hand whilst scouting for the cavalry that time. But he was never a for-Pete's-sake colonel and snow-white buckskins just ain't practical anywheres but on stage or the covers of a wild west magazine."

He washed down some pie with coffee he knew he'd need later before he added, "Jim Hickok was all right before Ned Buntline renamed him Wild Bill. He was the son of a preacher man. He first came to public notice along the Santa Fe Trail riding shotgun for the Overland

Stage. In '58, he and some other posse riders killed some Indian horse thieves. Later, along the Oregon Trail, Jim rightly or wrongly shot a gent they called McCanles, along with two sidekicks. Jim claimed it was self-defense. It might have been. After that, he rode for the north as a civilian scout in the western theater. Buntline has him acting as a sniper, a spy, and a heck of a hero. It's more certain he won a shoot-out over a card game with a tin-horn named Tutt in Springfield Missouri before he signed as a Deputy U.S. Marshal like me and got fired. After that, he worked hither and yon as town law. Then Jim shot a man named Phil Coe and one of own friends by mistake. By this time, he was the famous Wild Bill, on stage as such with Buffalo Bill in an act some laughed at in the wrong places."

Longarm shook his head wearily before adding, "He'd just married up with a bareback rider and circus owner called Agnes in Cincinnati and left her back East to see if they'd give him a job as the town marshal of Deadwood when the feeble-minded Cockeyed Jack shot him in the back for no sensible reason. Another local drunk they still call Calamity Jane has been saying ever since that they were fighting over *her*. You ladies are inclined to impute such motives to us menfolk no matter what we may say or do. Then Longarm added, "Finish your coffee. We've a train to catch, Miss Rowena."

She told him men *deserved* to be suspected of impure thoughts. He felt no call to go into what Calamity Jane looked like, off the covers of those Wild West magazines.

He paid their tab, left a dime at each of their places as they rose, and they went to gather her carpetbag and his saddle from the checkroom by the front door.

As they strolled up to Seventh Street and followed it east, they saw coal smoke rising ahead. When she got exited, he soothed, "When an engine's moving its smoke plume puffs like an Indian smoke signal. We're early. The train up from Denver's standing still and likely still unloading."

As they strode closer, they met others headed the opposite way as if to confirm Longarm's words. By the time they got to the terminal, the plank platform alongside the cars backed into the end of the line stood empty save for a couple of earlier arrivals headed the other way in hopes of getting a seat near the engine. It sounded wrong, but in summer with the train windows open, you caught more soot and fly ash through the same as you sat further *back* from the belching diamond stack of a straining locomotive. The exhaust steam feeding into the smoke chamber shot hot steaming smoke skyward to settle back down on the cars to the rear.

As Longarm and the gal with tea-colored hair moved along the now mostly empty cars, another experienced traveler, having let everyone else off first, decided it was time he got off, himself.

It made no nevermind to Longarm, at first, when the Fargo Kid swung his short self off betwixt two cars ahead. Longarm had never laid eyes on the squirt before and hadn't been been expecting trouble out of Denver from anything less than a six-foot-six amazon.

But he came unstuck, sudden, when the short and shabby stranger gasped, "You!" and went for his six-gun as, right *behind* Longarm and Rowena Burnes a deeper voice bellowed, "Son of a bitch!"

Longarm stiff-armed Rowena sideways off the platform. She landed on her shapely butt, in knee-high weeds, screaming fit to bust as two guns fired thunderous from opposite directions! Longarm rolled under the railroad car to his right, leaving his saddle and her carpetbag to shift for themselves as he rolled over to the other side across the dusty ballast to rise once more with his own six-gun in hand.

Nothing at all was taking place on his side of the parked

train. All sorts of noises were coming from the platform side. So Longarm went up the far steps of the nearest platform, crossed the same, and with considerable caution stuck his gun muzzle and bare face out the far side to see if he could tell what had just happened.

Rowena Burnes was back on her feet, wild-eyed and yelling, "Help! Police! Murder!" at the top of her voice. Nobody else was about to come any closer before, like Longarm, they figured out what the fuck all that gunplay had been about.

As Longarm looked up the platform toward the engine, he saw the short squirt who'd just scared the shit out of them sprawled limp as a rag doll on his back, smiling up at the cloudless sky as if it was an old pal. Nobody ever looked that dead unless they felt sincere about it.

Down the other way, toward the street, a larger form lay facedown, still gripping a Remington-Beals .44 in his outstretched gun hand. His dark Stetson had fallen off to one side and his exposed hair was black and curly.

Longarm dropped down, strode over, and rolled that corpse on its back. Then, he smiled thinly down at the oyster gray eyes staring blankly up from beneath bushy eyebrows meeting in the middle before he said, "Howdy, Crimp. Been looking high and low for you. Just lay still 'til I can get back to you, hear?"

He holstered his own six-gun and went to help Rowena back up on the platform, soothing, "It's over. You can stop screaming, now, Miss Rowena!"

She only calmed down enough to gasp, "Dear Lord! I thought they just shot me, front and back!"

He took her by the arms to shake her gently as he told her, "They weren't shooting at us. They were shooting at one another. They knew one another way better than I knew either of them, or vice versa."

As she calmed down, and neither body sprawled on the sun-silvered planks did another thing but leak a little, the more familiar figure of City Marshal Duggan in the flesh came along the platform, his own six-gun drawn, to dramatically demand some damned explaining.

Longarm pointed with his chin at the nearest cadaver to declare in a certain tone, "That one's Crimp Gooding, the mildly federal want I told you I was up this way about. He was on the dodge from a way more serious crook he'd turned in for bounty money. I ain't dead certain yet, but from the way they both reacted when they laid eyes on one another a few minutes ago, I'm going to be mighty puzzled if that shorter cuss yonder ain't the one and original Fargo Kid you may have heard about."

Marshal Duggan had. He marveled, "Do you mean to tell me we just caught that convicted murderer who carved up three men busting out of the Pueblo Jail?"

Longarm dryly remarked, "From where I was standing, it appears they caught one another. But I'll go along with your version if you'd care to take both bodies off my hands. I just hate paperwork, and anyone can see I had nothing to do with the death of either."

Rowena stayed put by their baggage as Longarm and the Leadville Law moved up the platform for a closer look at the smaller one. Since few, if any, escaped killers carry proof of their true identity on them, the two lawmen agreed no Denver public library card made out to one Rory O'Connor meant much. But Longarm said, "His real name was Tone Corrigan. I understand a King Rory O'Connor Don was the last native king of Ireland. He sure had a modest opinion of himself. But what the hell, the proof will be in the pudding as soon as someone from Pueblo arrives to have a look at him."

Marshal Duggan said, "My people told me about Rory O'Connor and the high court on Tara before the coming of the strangers. But whether this one's the Fargo Kid or some other gaboon, doesn't this mean your federal case is over, with Crimp Gooding dead and all and all?"

Longarm headed back to load Rowena and their baggage aboard the train as he said, "I surely hope so. We'll be leaving, now, since you'll be as able to explain your capture of the Fargo Kid without my help. As for whether it's over or not, at the risk of offending you with the words of an old Protestant church song, farther along we'll know more about it. Farther along we'll understand why. But in the meantime I may still have a six-foot-six amazon after my own ass!"

Chapter 20

There was nothing much to do but talk aboard a pokey narrow-gauge train so, by the time they rolled into Denver with the sun hanging low over the Front Range behind them, they both knew more about one another's problems than they might have ever asked.

Longarm didn't understand why so many women had him down as a soft-hearted sissy. Few *men* seemed to find him soft. But Rowena kept asking what-oh-what he'd ever do if that big bad Increase Younger ever caught up with him.

He dryly assured her, "I'll offer to take her to supper, and she'll take it wrong and run off screaming that I'm after her fair white body."

That worked. She didn't put up much of a fuss when he left their loads in the Denver baggage room of the I.C&SRR and took her to the nearest Chop Suey place. She confessed she'd never et Chinee before, and asked how they could be certain they weren't being served rats and cats or worse.

He ordered pork lo mein with egg *fu yung* for the both of them before he replied, "How do you know you ain't getting rats and cats or worse in a fancy French joint? I

177

know the folk here, which is more than I can say for lots of places I've et, and if you can't tell the taste of eggs and pork from rats and cats, you sure have rotten taste, no offense. Let's talk about that boarding house I mentioned, coming down the grade this afternoon. Like I said, room and board at eight bucks a week has the cheapest hotel in town beat when you factor in eating out. I know you have enough on you for two weeks room and board with some pocket jingle left over whilst you look for a job, and I know a lady who runs and empoyment agency where . . ."

"Have you brought *her* here for a Chinee supper, too?" she cut in.

He wrinkled his nose and said, "Well, sure I have. Anyone can see I'm the kind of chump who'd ask his ladylove to find a job for a way younger and better looking gal. You're as bad as my boss, Miss Rowena. *He* doubts my ability to show common sense around any woman, but, for the record, the married lady who runs that employment agency is in her not-too-well-preserved fifties, and we're pals because I cleared her boy when he was falsely accused of being somewhere he hadn't been, speaking of fool kids who wander astray."

The Chinee waiter brought their order on a tray and proceeded to share it out between them, grinning fit to bust. Longarm warned her to take tea with her grub instead of coffee, explaining how the Chinee had invented tea but still had a lot to learn about coffee.

Their waiter laughed like a tickled hyena and ran back to the kitchen to tell the others what Longarm had just said.

Rowena thoughtfully decided, "They *like* you here, Custis. Do you come here often?"

He said, "Only when I'm down this way at suppertime. I seem to have more Chinee pals out this way than I deserve. It ain't true they're *all* treacherous heathen ingrates. Some seem to remember favors, and during those race riots we had out this way a spell back, I had to do my duty as a sworn peace officer and uphold the U.S. Constitution. I don't know how many times I've tried to explain it to them Sons of Han, as they call themselves, but they will go on about my saving a few of 'em from them howling mobs stirred up by labor agitators."

"You see, you *are* a nice man, even though you're ashamed to show it!" she declared, beaming across the table at him.

He said, "Aw, mush. How do you like lo mein? Lo mein's the greasy noodles. The sort of gravy-soaked flap jacks are the *egg fu yung*."

She said, "They're both delicious. I never knew Chinese food was this good. I've always been afraid to try it. What if I try to find a job before my money runs out and find I've failed?"

He said, "You'll be no worse off than you'd be if you sold yourself by telegraph wire to a man you didn't really care for, like the poor gal in that sad song. At least you'll have *tried*, Miss Rowena. Folk who never try may feel *safer* than those who try. They might not know they've missed anything if they never try. Had you never tried this Chinee food, you'd have never known whether you liked it. I met an old-timer one time who'd never et nothing but oatmeal mush, morning, noon and night. He likely died believing that was all there was worth eating."

She decided she'd give that boarding house and his pals at that employment agency a try after all. He tore a sheet out of his pocket notebook and wrote the address down for her. Then, after supper—he'd never ordered that library paste Chinee ate for dessert a second time—Longarm walked Rowena on to the nearby boarding house, saw the motherly landlady seemed to cotton to her, and let them work things out as he went back to the LC&CSRR for their shit.

Having her carpetbag and his heavier saddle delivered

179

by a redcap with a dray, for pocket change, beat by half toting the load all over creation his ownself. So he never had to go back to the boarding house and had no call to. An innocent young thing that suspicious of men, who'd said she was looking for some man to watch over her and had opined that he was not as mean as most men, was not a gal Longarm wanted to mess with. Rio Rita had started up with that shit after he'd picked *her* up in a *saloon*, for Pete's sake.

Billy Vail's night letter had instructed him to report in as soon as he got back to town, day or night, so Longarm hopped a horse-drawn streetcar up Colfax Avenue to save climbing Capitol Hill and got off on Sherman to walk south across the statehouse grounds to the marshal's residence to the south. The night was no longer young enough to call on that certain young widow with light brown hair who lived a tad further down Sherman, damn it. She'd given him pure ned and asked if all the whores at Madame Gould's place had been too busy for him, that night, the last time he'd shown up after dark, and life was too short to waste any of it arguing on a front porch with a woman.

He found Billy Vail seated on *his* front porch in the gathering dusk, stinking up the darkness with one of his expensive but pungent cigars, by orders of the lady of the house.

As Longarm lit a cheroot in self-defense to join him, Vail sat like a monarch in a folding army chair. Longarm perched on the railing, as Vail said, " 'Bout time you got here! What in the fuck have you been up to, old son? Your wire pleading to pack it in and come on home said you'd given up on Crimp Gooding. The evening extra edition of the *Rocky Mountain News* says Mayor Tabor and Marshal Duggan caught the Fargo Kid at the Lead-ville Terminal of the LC&SRR after he killed Crimp Gooding like he said he would. Since the news service allowed the Fargo Kid had died resisting arrest, that leaves you as the only one who'd have been at that terminal at that time as a witness to be trusted as far as I could throw this house. So tell me, how'd you get them to take your shoot-out off your hands?"

Longarm chuckled fondly and replied, "Figured you'd want me to, seeing the Fargo Kid's jailbreak and his death threats against Gooding were matters for the Colorado courts and you'd just wired you no longer gave a shit about Gooding. But I'd be bragging if I said I shot it out with anybody."

He blew a modest smoke ring and continued, "They shot each other without my help. The Fargo Kid couldn't have had anything against me, and he was the one facing me when the shooting started. Gooding was walking behind me, likely anxious to board the same train out of town after I'd spooked him the night before."

Longarm felt no call to detail how Gooding had failed to recognize him from the rear, one tall man in a suit looking much like another in the company of a much more interesting figure.

Longarm went on, "I just crabbed out of their way when they both yelled at each other and slapped leather at the same time. They were both on the prod. They were both experienced shootists and the range was less than ten yards. So it's academic who drilled whom a split second sooner. They both hit where they'd aimed, smack through both breastbones. With both of them dead and the town law coming to take charge, I knew you'd want me to board the train that was fixing to leave for Denver, so I did."

"How did Horace Tabor get on the front page this evening?" asked Vail.

Longarm shrugged and replied, "How does he get into most everything these days? He's Marshal Duggan's boss. When Duggan ain't cutting notches in his gun grips, he's likely got his nose up the rosy red rectum of his boss."

Vail sighed and said, "I wish *I* could find help like that.

They say around the club Horace Tabor's aspiring to national office. Won't they have fun back in Washington with a man who plays *chandeliers*?"

Longarm smiled dubiously and said, "I'm sure he was joshing when those church folk asked him to pay for a chandelier, and he gave them enough for two, asking who'd be *playing* those chandeliers at First Methodist. Men who like to be famous say all sorts of things and pose over all the dead outlaws they can. Can I go, now, Boss? It's past my bedtime after a day on the LC&SRR too tedious to describe."

Vail smiled dirty and said, "My wife says that widow woman down the street is entertaining visitors from back East, but there's always the new barmaid at the Black Cat or, of course, that matron out to that orphan asylum. So go forth, my son, and take your beating like a man, for you've done . . . all right, I reckon, and things seem to be getting back to tedious."

As Longarm rose from the rail, Vail asked, "Were you still in Pueblo when that sheriff's deputy was killed?"

Longarm frowned down to reply, "Not hardly. Hadn't heard anybody in Pueblo had been killed. Did he have a name?"

Vail nodded and said, "Manx, Deputy Roy Manx. Ring any bells?"

Longarm shook his head and said, "Never met up with him. He wasn't one of the Pueblo lawmen I talked to. How come *that* wasn't in any of the papers, Billy?"

Vail said, "That's why I wondered whether it happened before or after you'd left Pueblo. The county covered the whole thing up for the sake of his children, seeing it would cost the county less to let their momma raise 'em, and Roy Manx had it coming."

Longarm cocked a brow to ask, "Might we be discussing one of them unwritten law affairs?"

Vail nodded and said, "That's how come I've only gotten the bare facts, this far along the peace officer's grape-vine. To save others needless worry about rumors of a thoroughly shot-up lawman, Pueblo County has let it be known, in confidence, what really happened."

"So what really happened?" Longarm asked.

Vail wrinked his nose in disgust and replied, "It seems the late Roy Manx had a mighty pretty young wife every-one liked and a roving eye for anything under a skirt. They say the slut she caught him in bed with was a big old cow who took it in the ass. His wife might not have caught 'em together if he hadn't bragged so much about all them French and Greek lessons he'd been getting, as often as twice a day just a skip and a holler from his place of work. But, hearing the gossip, his long-suffering wife tracked him to their love nest with a Hopkins and Allen .44-Short and busted in to catch 'em in the act. So she emptied the wheel into them, reloaded, and emptied it into them again before his pals at the nearby jail could respond to the muffled fusillade."

Longarm whistled softly and asked, "The other woman, too?"

Vail said, "The other woman most of all. The self-made Widow Manx was content to kill her husband once, but reloaded to shoot the gal he'd been screwing a lot, in the face. They say the poor drab's mother would have a tough time recognizing the remains, but nobody's come forward to claim 'em. So they'll likely wind up in Potter's Field out past the slag heaps. She'd given her name as Jones, James, something as phoney, when she hired the cottage near her married keeper's office. Gals like her wind up that way a lot, and since you say you hadn't heard about either of 'em, what the hell do *we* care?"

Longarm observed, "Seems a shame for any human be-ing to wind up in Potter's Field with nobody giving a shit. But, like you just said, it happens. Any word on that *other* wayward gal, Increase Younger, speaking of of lost souls?"

Vail shook his head and said, "She may not be lost no more. She may have reformed. She sure as shit ain't in *Denver* these days. I suspect that once she'd sent you that dumb letter in Kansas City she met up with somebody she found more interesting, made up for ten lost years without a good screwing to settle her nerves, and decided feeling as free as a bird and as horny as rabbit had further adventures along the owlhoot trail beat. We'll never know for certain unless she fucks up again, of course."

"Then we're just going to *drop* the whole shebang?" Longarm asked in a hopeful tone.

Billy Vail replied in an expansive tone, "Why not? We never do dot every *i* and cross every *t* when we *catch* somebody, and, in this case, we don't seem to have anyone we really want to *catch*. It happens that way, old son. Make sure you show up for work on time, come morning."

Longarm said good night and left without making promises before he was certain where he'd be waking up the next morning. Heading up to the corner to follow the nearer Fourteenth Avenue downslope to the boundless opportunities of a Denver night, he saw a handsome team drawing a shiny black Berlin carriage headed the other way. He didn't care. But as the Berlin passed him, the coachman suddenly reined in and a familiar voice trilled out, "Custis Long! What's got into you this evening? Why are you walking the wrong way on my street, you big silly?"

As he strode back to the Berlin, tipping his hat brim to the gal with light brown hair sticking her head out at him, he told her he'd heard she had company.

The rich young widow trilled, "I just put them on an eastbound train at the Union Station. Where have you been the past few days? Someone told me you were out of town on a field mission."

Longarm said that was about the size of it. So she invited him to just climb aboard and tell her all about it.

So he did. And Billy Vail was sore as hell when he showed up so late for work the next morning.

LONGARM

Explore the exciting Old West with one of the men who made it wild!

J. R. ROBERTS
THE GUNSMITH